A Woman's Revenge

MAY 13

CH

A Woman's Revenge

Sherri L. Lewis, Rhonda McKnight,

and E.N. Joy

www.urbanchristianonline.com

Urban Books, LLC
78 East Industry Court
Deer Park, NY 11729

ISBN 13: 978-1-60162-747-6
ISBN 10: 1-60162-747-5

First Printing April 2013
Printed in the United States of America

10 9 8 7 6 5 4 3 2 1

Distributed by Kensington Corp.
Submit Wholesale Orders to:
Kensington Publishing Corp.
C/O Penguin Group (USA) Inc.
Attention: Order Processing
405 Murray Hill Parkway
East Rutherford, NJ 07073-2316
Phone: 1-800-526-0275
Fax: 1-800-227-9604

A Woman's Revenge

Sherri L. Lewis, Rhonda McKnight,
and E.N. Joy

The Sweet Taste of Revenge

Sherri L. Lewis

Chapter One

Sabrina Rogers, will you marry me?

I stared down at the huge rock on my finger, reliving those words being whispered into my ear. My ring sparkled in the moonlight shining through the sunroof overhead. Maybe if I kept looking at it, I would actually believe he proposed. We had only been seeing each other for five months. I had been working for Blake Harrison for almost a year, but the romance hadn't been going on long enough for me to expect this.

"We should be able to get those briefs over to you first thing Monday morning. One sec, let me check with my assistant. Yeah, I know. Late Friday night at the office." Blake put his Bluetooth on hold and turned to me. "The briefs for the Connor case. They're ready?"

I nodded. "Of course."

He smiled and winked at me. "That's my girl. I can always count on you." He clicked his Bluetooth back on. "Yeah, Monday morning first thing. Oh, and the Foster deposition . . ."

I smiled. Yeah, he could always count on me. I was the best executive assistant at West and Brunson Law Firm and now I was going to become the best wife. As soon as I helped him make partner, we would get married and I wouldn't have to work another day in my life.

"Almost home, sweetie." He glanced over at me. "Only about thirty more minutes."

"I'm okay, honey."

He switched hands on the steering wheel and reached over to caress my ring finger. "Yeah, I bet you are."

I lay back on the headrest. Daydreams of living in his penthouse condo on Sixteenth Street kept my mind off the long drive from Reston, Virginia back to Silver Spring, Maryland. It was the first time in a long time that I didn't pout the whole way home. It would only be a matter of months until Blake and I didn't have to drive to the next state just to go out to dinner. At least he was taking me out instead of me having to sneak up the back elevator to his place. All the secrecy still bothered me, but I had decided that it was a small price to pay for the wonderful life I was about to start living.

When we got back to my apartment complex, Blake pulled up next to my car. I knew our good-bye would be quick as always since we couldn't chance being seen in my parking lot together.

He walked around to my side of the car and opened it for me. I took his extended hand and, with one sweep, he pulled me into his arms. He planted a soft kiss on my lips. "So do I get to come upstairs tonight?"

I pulled back a little, but not out of his arms. "You know the rule. No nookie until I get the ring."

He held up my left hand. "What do you call this thing on your finger?"

I laughed and pushed him away. "I mean the wedding ring, silly. This is the engagement ring."

He clenched his jaw. "Stop playing games, Sabrina."

I saw a bit of anger flash across his face. I had seen the same look in his eyes when he got really mad at work. For a second, I felt nervous.

"I'm not playing games, Blakey." I put the sweetest, most innocent look on my face and stroked a finger across his cheek. "You know I'm a church girl and you ain't getting none before we say 'I do.'"

His jaw loosened only a little.

"Remember, that's what you love about me. I'm the good Christian girl who reminds you of your mama."

The smile came back across his face. "Yes, that is what I love about you." He kissed me on the nose. "I don't think I've ever met a woman as pure and innocent as you, Sabrina Rogers." He gave me that intense admiring look of his that made me know for sure that what everybody said about us was wrong. Blake really did love me.

He handed me a blue ring box. "This is for you to keep the ring in. You wouldn't want to lose it, much as I paid for it."

I took the box and gave him a confused look.

He let out a heavy sigh. "Come on, Sabrina. You know you can't wear it to work. How would you explain it? No one can know we're engaged yet."

"But—"

"But what? If Brunson's assistant asks you who you're engaged to, what are you going to tell her? The last thing we need is that nosy broad all up in our business."

He was right. Paris could get some juicy information first thing in the morning, and by the end of the day, every person in every department of our huge office would know about it.

"I can't have anything affecting this decision. There's no one as qualified as me or who works as hard as me in that whole office. Who else could they even be considering for partner?" Blake tilted my chin upward to put one last kiss on my lips. "It'll only be a few more months, honey. And then the whole world will know. Can you be a little more patient with me?"

I gave him a reassuring smile and nodded.

"That's my girl."

I watched him drive away in his Mercedes S-Class and looked over at my own car. Pretty soon, I wouldn't be driving a Toyota Corolla anymore. I tried to imagine what kind of car he would buy me. A man like Blake Harrison wouldn't have his wife driving around town in just any old thing.

I glanced at my car again and noticed an envelope on the windshield. My name was typed in large, bold print across the front of it. I pulled it out from under the wiper blade, looking over my shoulder, wondering who could have put it there. I tucked it under my arm and practically floated up the steps into my apartment. *What kind of wedding dress will I wear? Where will we get married? We might as well run off and get married because I have no family and Blake isn't really connected to his. We could have the ceremony and our honeymoon on an exotic island somewhere. That would be exciting.* I had barely been out of Maryland before, let alone to another country.

I looked around my apartment. It had served me well, but I was looking forward to getting out of here for good. I'd get rid of all my furniture the day before I said "I do." None of my Walmart, Target, and, on a good day, IKEA specials were good enough for Sixteenth Street.

I laid the envelope on my breakfast room table and danced around the kitchen for a few minutes. I was going to be Mrs. Blake Harrison. I'd have a maid to clean my house and wash my clothes. I'd have a cook to prepare our gourmet meals. I wouldn't have to buy no-name brands from the grocery store ever again.

I sashayed back to my bedroom and threw open my closet, wrinkling my nose at my T.J.Maxx, Ross, and Marshall's wardrobe. Soon, I'd wear only the finest designer clothes and shoes—and not from an off-the-rack store either. Maybe I'd even have my clothes specially made for me by my own personal tailor.

I flopped back onto my bed and held my left hand up in the air, admiring my ring. What would we name our children? Blake Jr., of course, would be our son. And hopefully he'd let me name our daughter after my grandmother. Although Bessie wasn't very rich sounding. Maybe her middle name could be Bessette or something like that.

I lay there for a few minutes, daydreaming about my glorious future. As my eyes fluttered shut, the sight of the mysterious envelope sitting on my table drifted into my mind. I had forgotten all about it. I couldn't imagine who had left it. Curiosity got the best of me, so I hopped up off the bed and did a little princess dance down the hall to get it. I skipped back down the hall to my bedroom and plopped onto the bed to open it. I sat there with it pressed to my chest for a few minutes, try-ing to imagine what was inside.

Maybe it was a surprise from Blake. Like a trip to the spa or a gift certificate to Macy's or something. Yeah, that was it. *He must have had a courier bring it over while we were out to dinner.*

I carefully opened the envelope, wanting to preserve it and whatever was inside for my keepsake box. A let-ter typed in that same bold font on expensive station-ary fell out.

It opened with four words that made my heart stop:

HE'S CHEATING ON US!

Chapter Two

Last night, I should have had the sweetest sleep of my life, filled with dreams of the prosperous new life I was going to live. Instead, I was awake the whole night with the contents of that letter flashing through my mind.

The opening sentence alone was bad enough. Not only did it say that the love of my life was cheating on me. The fact that she said "us" hinted that there was more than one "other woman."

My first thought was to ignore the whole thing. Blake was an amazing man any woman would want. I was sure that some jealous hoochie who had her sights on him was plotting how to get rid of me so she could have him for herself.

But as I read the rest of the letter I realized that this woman—whoever she was—knew intimate details about Blake that only someone close to him would have known.

She mentioned a lot of general stuff like his clothing and shoes sizes, his suit preferences, and his precious watch collection. Anybody doing a little research could figure that stuff out. Then she mentioned all his favorite foods and exactly how he liked them prepared. Blake was so particular about everything down to the brand of food he had to have. But still, somebody could have gotten that information from his cook.

I thought I got worried the most when she mentioned the things that made him mad and the things that made him happy. She wrote about how he did that funny, jagged breathing thing when he was tired and about to fall asleep. And how he liked weird sports like lacrosse and rugby. According to her, he liked it when she rubbed his head and massaged his neck, just like he did when I did it. But then again, that could be any man.

She mentioned several other embarrassing things that I didn't even want to think about: the sounds he made during sex, what he liked to do after sex, and how he liked to have sex. I skipped the lines that had specific information about his private parts. Since I had never seen Blake naked or had sex with him, I would have to take her word for it.

Everything she said put just enough doubt in my mind that I had to know the truth. I had no other choice but to follow the directions in the letter and meet her.

I put on my nicest suit, plenty of concealer to cover the bags under my eyes, and my Jimmy Choo pumps I had bought myself as a gift from Blake. I needed to look the part of the fiancée of one of the city's high-powered lawyers, not the part of a young girl who had started out as an administrative assistant in his law firm two and a half years ago.

I sat at the table in the restaurant, trying to keep from shaking my leg and biting my nails, for fifteen minutes before a woman walked up to the table. My heart raced as she sat down across from me.

My mouth fell open. We could pass for sisters. Same smooth brown skin, almond-shaped eyes, high cheekbones, narrow nose, and thick, full lips. She wore her thick, long hair in wavy curls while I kept mine pulled back in a bun at the nape of my neck. She was a little thicker than my size four but in a sexy, curvy way. Made me feel skinny.

The corners of her mouth turned upward. "Yeah. It's almost like looking in a mirror, isn't it? Close your mouth, sweetie. You ain't seen nothing yet."

My attempts at looking classy were no match for this lady. She had on an expensive-looking, tailor-fitted, business-blue pantsuit accented with real silver jewelry. She carried a large leather Coach briefcase that matched her Italian leather shoes. The restaurant she had picked for us to meet in was one where I would never order anything more than water. Maybe an appetizer if Blake had slipped me a little extra change. Her level of class, sophistication, and elegance made me feel like a little girl fighting way out of my league.

She glanced down at my folded hands on the table. "Nice ring."

I looked down at the rock on my finger and forgot I wasn't supposed to smile. "Yeah, he proposed last night." I held it up to let her know that, in spite of her class and beauty, I was the one Blake Harrison had chosen. Whatever claims she was here to make meant nothing next to this ring.

When I looked across the table, she was holding up her left hand. Her third finger sported a ring identical to mine. My mouth dropped open again. For some reason, that made her laugh. She sounded more bitter than amused.

She laid a large manila envelope on the table in front of me. I started to reach for it, but stopped. I was sure I didn't want to see what was inside. "Who are you, and how did you get this information about my Blake?"

"*Your* Blake?" She scoffed. "Aren't you sweet. How old are you anyway? You don't look like you could be a day over twenty-one."

I sat up in my chair. "I'm twenty-five."

"The youngest one yet," she said with a smirk on her lips that made me feel five years old. She slid her sunglasses off her face and I could tell that she had tried to hide the puffiness in her eyes with makeup too. In spite of her elegance and maturity, it seemed like she was as hurt by all this as I was.

"We range in age from twenty-five to forty-one. Range in size from two to twelve. We all have the same face, though." She peeked around at my bun. "Same long, thick hair. One thing I can say for Blake Harrison. He's consistent."

My mouth went dry and my palms started to sweat. There wasn't a day that went by that I didn't say that same thing about Blake. His middle name was consistent.

"You know, when I first found out about the others, I figured he was just getting his last flings in before the wedding. I figured I'd let him play and get it out of his system. But then when I found out he had bought another engagement ring . . . I realized there was a real problem."

I stared at her for a second. *Let him get it out of his system?* She sounded crazy. I couldn't imagine Blake being in a relationship with someone like that. Maybe she was some lunatic stalker trying to get him away from me. "Why should I believe you? How do I know that you're not . . . just a—"

"You don't have to believe me." She pushed the envelope on the table closer to me. "I came with proof. Open it up. Take a look at the rest of us."

I stared into that face that looked just like mine and then down at the ring on her finger, feeling all my hopes and dreams dissolving into a puddle on the ground. Sixteenth Street suddenly felt very far away. I fingered the envelope, but still wasn't ready to open it. "How . . . how many are there?"

She rolled her eyes and picked up the envelope. "Here, let me show you."

I thought I would choke on the water the waitress had just brought to the table when she pulled out a thick stack of photos. My eyes must have been huge because she looked at me and I could see pity on her face. "You sure you're ready for this?"

I shook my head and looked down at the table. She reached across and put a hand on top of mine. "Is this your first time being in love, honey?"

I nodded and tried to squeeze back the tears starting to fall down my face. I hadn't planned on coming here and crying like a baby in front of my fiancé's mistress. Or, should I say, my fiancé's other fiancée.

"I'm Christine, by the way." She passed me a napkin and waited for a second until I pulled myself together. "We don't have to do this. You don't have to see the pictures, I mean. You can just take my word for it and walk away from him."

Yeah, that's exactly what she wanted me to do. Walk away from Blake so she could have him. I shook my head and wiped the last of the tears away from my eyes. No way was I going to disappear that easy. She was going to have to prove that she was more than some tramp trying to steal my man. "No. I want to see."

"Okay then." Christine got up and sat in the chair next to mine.

The first picture she pulled out was of her and Blake hugged up together on what looked like the deck of one of those dinner cruise ships. She was all smiles holding her ring up next to her face. "This was the night of our engagement at the harbor. Three months ago."

Her eyes went soft for a second as she stared at the two of them, looking as happy in that picture as Blake and I must have looked last night. Her face got hard again real quick as she called Blake a name I would never let cross my lips.

I said, "So he takes you to Baltimore. He takes me down to Reston." *Blake must have wanted to keep her a secret, just like me.*

She frowned. "Takes me to Baltimore? I *live* in Baltimore. You mean he drives you an hour and a half away to take you out to dinner?" She laughed that bitter laugh again. "You poor girl." She gave me such a condescending look I shrunk down in my seat some.

The next picture was a black-and-white and had been taken from a distance. It was another woman who looked like us. Her head was thrown back as she laughed at whatever Blake was whispering in her ear. A third picture had another woman who looked like us but she looked a little older and a little thicker. She was smiling real hard with Blake's lips close to her ear. I looked away quickly, my heart pounding in my chest. "Where did you . . . How did you . . ."

"Private investigator." She looked into my eyes. "You okay?"

I shook my head slowly.

"First time you been cheated on?"

I nodded.

Christine patted my hand. "Sweetie, I wish I could tell you this was going to be the last. All men cheat. It's just their nature. Poor things just can't help themselves." She shook her head, eyeing the pictures. "I've never seen it this bad, though."

I looked at her and figured she had to be in her early thirties. The look in her eyes said she had been through a lot. The tone in her voice said this kind of hurt and heartbreak weren't new to her. "Why? Why would he . . . Why do they?" I asked.

She stared at me like I was from another planet. "Are you serious?"

I nodded and looked away. I didn't believe that all men cheated. Maybe that was her experience, but they couldn't be *all* bad. Maybe I could figure out from her how to know which ones would cheat and what made them cheat. Even though my heart felt like someone had just driven over it with a truck, I still wanted to get married and have a family one day. It was the only thing I had ever wanted, since I didn't have a real family growing up.

"I'm going to give you this for free." She fanned the pictures out. "Why men cheat." She chuckled to herself. After she shuffled a couple of the photos around, she organized them into little stacks. "Sometimes it's because they're bored or feel like they're not getting what they need from the relationship." She arranged the stacks in order on the table. I was shocked to see pictures of Blake with his arms wrapped around me behind his locked office door. I thought we had been discreet. *How did someone get pictures of us at work?*

Christine continued, her voice getting angrier as she kept talking. "Some men cheat because they can't find everything they want in one woman. So they get what they need from several women. Looks like Blake has a wide range of interests and tastes he's trying to feed with a bunch of women."

She stopped shuffling the pictures and took a big sip of water. "Ready? Let's take a look at the many faces of Blake Harrison." She pointed to her own picture. "I'm a lawyer, like Blake. Truth be told, I'm actually smarter than Blake. So I fulfill his need for a brilliant woman who can challenge his intellect."

She picked up the first stack of photos, all of Blake and the same woman. Her makeup and clothes were real dramatic looking, and even though the pictures were taken secretly, she looked like she was on stage or something. Like the world was watching her. She had to be almost six feet tall because she was almost as tall as Blake, who was six foot two.

Christine said, "This one lives in New York and is an aspiring singer, model, and actress. I guess she fulfills his artistic side."

My eyes bugged out when I looked at the next stack of pictures. The girl had on a tight tank top with her breasts spilling out of it, and super tight jeans. She looked like me, Christine, and the New York model lady except for the blond wig she was wearing. What was really crazy was Blake's outfit. Most days he wore thousand-dollar suits. The most casual thing I had ever seen him wear was Dockers and a button-down shirt. In this picture, he had on an oversized jersey with a baseball cap, Tims, and jeans.

"Who knew Blake had a little thug in him?" Christine chuckled. "This one lives in Philly."

She looked me up and down. "Let me guess. Not only are you his personal assistant who waits on him hand and foot, you're the sweet little church girl who reminds him of his blessed mama—God rest her soul."

"Executive assistant," I said with not enough fire in my voice. It felt like she had stabbed me in the heart.

The waitress came to take our food order but I knew there was no way I could eat. I was ready to throw up the little bit of water I drank looking at the pictures scattered across the table.

"Well, if it makes you feel any better, you and I were the only ones who graduated to fiancée," Christine said. "The model and the Philly girl seem to be random weekend flings."

I thought of the hotel, limo, and train reservations I had made for those weekend flings that I had thought to be business trips. My stomach turned. What kind of man had his woman make his travel arrangements to go sleep with his other women?

"The only one I can't figure out is the older lady." She pushed the other pictures to the side and fanned out three pictures. "I would say she's filling his mother hunger, but even though this chick is forty-one, she doesn't look like anybody's mama. And judging from the fact that my PI said most of their time together was spent having loud sex, she don't act like nobody's mama either. They live in the same building. Maybe she was just a convenient piece of tail. Maybe she did all the freaky stuff I refused to do."

My face turned red with embarrassment at her talking about sex so openly. "Well, at least I never had sex with him." For a brief second, I felt a little better. It was my only consolation in this whole mess.

For the first time since the whole conversation started, Christine's mouth dropped open and she looked shocked. "Never had sex with him?"

I shook my head with a sense of pride that I had more dignity in this whole thing than she did.

A broad grin spread across her face. "Then, honey, you missed out on the best part of Blake Harrison." She let out a laugh so loud several other people in the restaurant turned to look at us. When Christine stopped laughing, she placed a hand on my cheek. "You poor, sweet child. Promise me one thing. Next time you'll deal with a man your own age?"

My cheeks went red again. I looked down at the table.

She sat back in her chair and downed the glass of wine the waitress had brought at her request. She slammed the glass down on the table so hard I thought it would break.

"Remember this." She gave me a serious look. "When you wade through all that bull crap and get to the root of the matter . . . Why do men cheat? Because they can."

I pulled the stacks of pictures toward me, wanting to burn each one of them into my brain to give me the strength to do what I needed to do the next time I saw Blake Harrison. The pictures of the older lady were farthest away and I strained to see her.

Christine saw me looking and slid them toward me. "Yeah, take a good look. You can see how fabulous you'll be sixteen years from now."

I picked up the pictures, staring into the older, thicker woman's beautiful face. I closed my eyes, shook my head, and stared at them again. I let out a gasping breath.

It couldn't be. I looked at the last picture that gave it away. As seemed to be his habit, Blake was whispering something in her ear. With her head thrown back, mouth wide open, I could almost hear that familiar laugh bellowing out. I hadn't heard it in more than ten years, but it was a sound I could never forget.

I started shaking so hard I dropped all the pictures. Christine picked them up, shoved them into the envelope, and then stared at me with concern in your eyes. "What's wrong, honey? Are you okay?"

I shook my head and could barely get the words out. "That's . . . that's my mother."

Chapter Three

I honestly didn't know how I made it back to my apartment. After I recognized that face in those photos, I got up and took off running. Christine called out after me, but I just kept running until I didn't hear her voice anymore. I didn't remember getting in my car or starting it up or driving the twenty-minute drive home.

I sat in my car parked in front of my apartment and finally broke down. I didn't know what tore me up the most: finding out who Blake Harrison really was or finding out that my so-called fiancé had slept with my . . . mother.

I screamed out loud and banged both fists on the steering wheel. I thought I hated her as much as I could hate any person before, but now I felt new levels of hate rising up in me. My grandmother had always warned me that my hate for my mother would eat me up one day and right now I believed it would. I knew, sure as I was black—as Grandma used to say—if I saw her right now, I would kill her.

I kept screaming and banging until my head hurt and my voice was raw. It never occurred to me that someone might hear me or see me. If they did, I was surely gonna get carried off to the crazy house.

Maybe that's where I belonged. Because I was crazy to believe that someone like Blake Harrison could have actually loved me and wanted to marry me. That thought had crossed my mind so many times during our whirlwind romance. Why would someone like him pick someone like me? I had thought it was God's blessing.

I let out another scream. This was no blessing. It was a curse.

There was a soft knock on the passenger's side window. I looked through my swollen eyes to see who it was. *Just when I didn't think this situation could get any worse. . . .*

It was Gerald Dawson, one of my neighbors. He had taken me out to dinner a few times and to a few movies. We had even gone to church together and out for Sunday brunch afterward. He was a really sweet guy and I actually had enjoyed our dates, but when Blake first expressed an interest in me, I dropped Gerald like a hot potato. A simple guy like him didn't hold a candle to a man like Blake, so I dismissed him without a second thought. I guess this was divine justice: him getting to see me all torn up over Blake a few months after I hurt his feelings.

He knocked again. "Sabrina, you okay?"

I dug in my purse and found some old, crumbly tissue and dried my face. I tried to wave him away, but he came around to my side of the car and opened the door. "What's going on? Is everything all right?"

"I'm fine. Please, just go away."

"You don't look fine. Is there anything I can help you with? Did someone die or something?" He was so doggone sweet, just like he had been every time we went out. Made me feel even worse. The tears started flowing again and I dropped my head onto the steering wheel.

"No. Nothing like that."

"Okay." He shifted from side to side for a second. "Is there anyone I can call for you? I hate leaving you alone like this."

"No. Please just go." I made myself smile at him. "I'm fine. Really."

"Okay. Well if you need anything call me. You still have my number?" His eyes were hopeful.

I nodded. I couldn't tell him I had deleted his number from my phone after my third date with Blake. "Thanks, Gerald."

He patted me on the shoulder and left.

Somehow I dragged myself into my apartment. I closed the door and leaned back on it, crying real hard at the thought that there really was no one he could call for me.

I lost my best friend, Janine, over an argument we had when I confided in her about my relationship with Blake. She had said a bunch of stuff that I thought was mean and jealous then, but I now knew to be the truth. She had apologized and tried to make up, but I had dissed her too, looking forward to the new set of classier friends I would have in Blake Harrison's world.

Janine still called me once a week—every week—and left the sweetest messages about how much she loved me, inviting me to go places and hang out with her. I always ignored her, thinking she'd get the picture, but every week, right on schedule, her name would show up on my caller ID. The rest of our circle of friends didn't take so kindly to being ignored and had stopped calling. There was no way I could call any of them now.

I hadn't been to church in months. I worked so hard for Blake during the week that I needed Sundays off to rest. It was wrong, but I figured I'd have time for God later when I was married, well off, and didn't need to work anymore.

I cried all the way down the hall to my bedroom, peeled off my suit, and crawled into bed. I prayed for sleep but all sorts of thoughts kept creeping into my mind. Those brown, beautiful faces flashed through my mind, one by one. How had Blake managed to juggle all of us? I guessed I was his Friday evening girl. He must have gone to Baltimore on Saturdays and Sundays. He had his occasional weekend trips to Philly and New York. And then my mother . . .

I screamed so hard I was sure my neighbors would call the police because they thought someone was trying to kill me. I cried until my voice was ragged. When I finally quieted down to occasional sniffles and sobs, my cell phone chimed to let me know a text message had come through. It was from Blake:

> Dinner plans at the club got cancelled so you can come over for a nice dinner with your future husband. Remember to use the service elevator.

Dinner plans got cancelled? I bet they did. I was sure he had planned to be in Baltimore with Christine. So since she had cancelled, I was supposed to drop everything and go have dinner with him? Did he make Christine the lawyer use the service elevator?

I threw the cell phone across the room. It hit the wall with a loud bang and then fell into pieces on the floor. Next thing I knew, I had jumped out of bed and thrown on some jeans and a top. After I pulled on my tennis shoes, I ran toward the kitchen and started pulling open drawers.

Blake knew me as the little innocent church girl. He didn't know that before I got all saved and holy, I was raised by a mother who would cut a man real good without thinking twice. I had seen her stuff a butcher knife in her purse many a time before she'd go running out the door, yelling some guy's name mixed with a bunch of cuss words. She'd come home, calmly wash the knife, and put it back in the kitchen drawer. All she would say was, "Sometimes, a woman just has to let a man know . . ."

It was only after my mother ran off and left me that my grandmother started taking me to church. Grandma said she couldn't have me turning out like my mother—being wild, getting pregnant, and leaving her with another child to raise.

I shoved a couple of kitchen knives into my purse. I wasn't sure what I was going to slash, but something was going to get cut tonight. *Maybe Blake's pretty-boy face.*

I got in my car and headed for Sixteenth Street. I pushed God's voice out of my head. I was gonna get Blake Harrison and I was gonna get him good. I had to push my grandmother's voice out of my head, too. Because with those knives in my purse and revenge in my heart toward some man, I was becoming something she never wanted me to be.

Just like my mother.

Chapter Four

As I pulled up to Blake's building, I saw Christine driving off in a Lexus coupe with a smile on her face. *What was she doing here? Did she just confront Blake?* No way would I be smiling after getting up in his face. And there was surely no way he would be smiling when I left.

My first inclination was to proudly march up to the concierge and tell him to unlock the elevator up to the penthouse so I could make a grand entrance. I thought about the knives in my purse, though. I didn't know what damage I would do when I got upstairs and didn't need anyone identifying my picture as the last person seen going to Blake Harrison's condo when the police started their investigation.

I drove around to the service entrance and prepared to go up the back elevator like I always did. The problem was, I usually used the service elevator to ride up to the floor beneath his, and then would call from my cell phone for him to come down to get me since I had to have a special key to get up to the penthouse. Unfortunately, my cell phone was lying in pieces on my bedroom floor.

When I thought of the covert shenanigans I had let Blake take me through for the sake of "discretion," as he called it, my blood boiled hotter. I got off at the floor beneath his and started pacing back and forth, trying to figure out how me and my knives were going to get upstairs. I paced up the back hall, and then to the main hall where the front elevator was.

As I tromped by the fancy wallpaper and light fixtures in the hallway, staring down at the fancy carpet, I realized how nice and high class this building was. I would probably never get to live anywhere this nice. I would be stuck in my low-class apartment for the rest of my life.

And then it really hit me. I was about to lose everything. Not only had I lost my fiancé, I was about to lose my job. There was no way I could continue to be his executive assistant. I wouldn't be able to work in the same building. There was no way I could be anywhere near that man.

Where would I find a job that paid me the inflated salary that Blake paid me? I'd have to go back to my one bedroom in the same complex I had upgraded from last year when I got the promotion and raise after switching from lowly secretary to Blake's executive assistant.

I stopped cold in the hallway when I realized I had given up everything for him—going back to college, my friends, my church. Now I had nothing.

And now I was going to take everything from him. I would plunge my knife straight through his heart, just like he had plunged a knife through mine. Did he really think he was going to get away with this?

I heard the elevator ding behind me and heard someone get off. I hoped they were going toward the opposite end of the building from where I was pacing. If a witness mentioned seeing me pacing on the floor below Blake's, I could get a life sentence or the death penalty because they could say his death was premeditated.

Chill out, Sabrina. You're not gonna kill the man. He just needs to be shook up a little. Maybe shed a few drops of blood.

I waited until I heard the person stick their key in their door, open it, and go inside. When the door closed behind them, I slowly tiptoed back down the hall. Just as I was about to pass the door, it swung open and the person stepped out, directly into my path.

Her eyes flew open at the same time mine did. I stood staring into her face. She stood there, staring back at mine.

"Sabrina?" she finally said.

I nodded. "Mama . . ."

Chapter Five

"Or should I say Roxie." I called my mother by her first name as I always had. We stood there staring at each other for what felt like hours. I was paralyzed by shock and anger. She looked surprised and guilty.

I looked down at her hands. One held a manila envelope with her name, Roxanne St. James, typed in a familiar bold font. The other hand held a familiar stack of pictures. The picture of Blake hugging me in his office was on top.

So Christine had left here from meeting with Roxie, rather than confronting Blake.

"Sabrina . . . I . . ." Roxie looked down at the photo and up at me with this sad look in her eyes. She reached out a hand to touch my face.

"Don't you dare touch me." I slapped her hand away.

She looked up and down the hall. "Sabrina, I had no idea—"

"Don't you even talk to me!" My voice was growing louder.

"Keep your voice down, young lady. Do you want—"

I snapped. I gathered up all the hatred I had for her from the last twelve years and mixed it with the hatred I now had for Blake and lunged at her. She dropped the pictures, grabbed my arm, and jerked me inside her condo. She closed the door behind her.

I screamed and lunged at her again. Roxie dodged out of my way and I ended up hitting the door. I felt my wrist slam and pain shot up my arm, which made me even madder. I reached into my purse and pulled out the larger of the two knives and lunged at her again.

I found myself on the ground, face down, with Roxie's hand gripping my bruised wrist and her knee in the middle of my back. "Have you lost your got-durned mind?" Her smoky voice uttered the phrase my grandmother used to use on those early mornings when Roxie came sneaking in the house from doing God knows what in the streets all night.

Her words stilled me for a second, then broke me. I let out one last scream. "I hate you I hate you I hate you I hate you . . ."

I burst into loud sobs, lying right there in the middle of her foyer floor. Roxie slowly pulled the knife out of my hand and I lay there, face down, crying for what seemed like forever. It was all too much: finding out the truth about Blake, realizing I was losing everything, then running smack dab into the one person I hated on Planet Earth with everything in me. It was enough to make me lose my mind.

I finally sat up and dragged myself over to the door and lay back against it.

Roxie peered at my face. "For years, I've *dreamed* of the day when I would get to see you again." She let out a low chuckle. "I have to say, this isn't quite how I imagined it would be."

I reached into my purse, fishing for the other knife. Maybe, just maybe, I would have good enough aim to put it through her eyeball.

She held up the knife. "Looking for this?" She shook her head, a perplexed look on her face. "Did you come over here to kill me?"

I gritted my teeth. "No. I came over here to cut Blake. You were going to be a bonus. A *big* bonus."

She chuckled again. "Wow. And Christine said you were a sweet little innocent church girl. You certainly had her fooled."

"I was a sweet little innocent church girl until I found out that my fiancé had been sleeping with my long-lost mother."

The laughter left her eyes and a pained look appeared in them. "Sabrina, honey, I'm so sorry about all this. I didn't know you and Blake . . . I never meant to hurt you."

It was my turn to laugh. "Never meant to hurt me? Really? Since when? Since when did you start to care even a little bit about the way I felt?"

She opened her mouth to protest but then bit her lip. She let out a deep breath. "It wasn't that I didn't care. I always cared. It was just that—"

"Save it, Roxie. 'Cause I don't care anymore either."

We sat there in silence for a few minutes, me with my anger and hatred, her with her guilt and regrets.

She finally spoke. "So if you were here to cut him, what were you doing on my floor? How did you even know where I lived? Christine said she didn't give you that information."

"She told me you lived in the building. I didn't know this was your floor. I came up here because I was trying to . . ." There was no way I was going to let her further humiliate me by letting her know I had no direct access to the penthouse.

She pursed her lips and I knew she knew. I pushed myself up off the floor and picked up my purse. All the fire I had in me had drained out and now I only wanted to go home and get in my bed. I wanted to sleep until they evicted me from my apartment. Or maybe I would just sleep until I died.

Roxie held the knives out toward me. "I could get you upstairs. But honestly, a stabbing would be too kind for a man like Blake Harrison. He needs to die a slow, painful death."

"How?" I took the knives out of her hand and shoved them back into my purse.

She narrowed her eyes and pressed her lips together, thinking. "Yes. That is the question."

She spun on her heels and walked farther into her apartment. Intrigued by any thoughts she had on how to make Blake suffer, I followed her.

My mouth gaped as I entered her living area. It was a beautiful space, elegantly decorated. She had a creamy white leather sofa and loveseat with a thick, white area rug covering her polished hardwood floors. She had what looked like expensive art and exotic-looking foreign stuff she probably had bought on her travels all over the world.

"Looks like Mr. St. James actually taught you some class, Roxie. You really came up in the world. Where is he by the way? Did you run off and abandon him, too?"

She rubbed her hands together, staring down at the floor. "I guess I deserve that. My husband died five years ago."

I guessed I was supposed to say I was sorry, but I wasn't. The only person I hated more than Roxie was the man who had stolen her away from me. Who had rejected me as his daughter and forced my mother to choose which one of us she loved more. He had won twelve years ago and I had hated him since.

She stood there looking like she wanted to apologize again. Before she could open her mouth, I spoke. "So, a slow, painful death. What's your plan?"

It was the only reason I was still here. I didn't want to go back and hash out things from our past. I didn't want her to apologize and explain and ask forgiveness. I just wanted to make Blake Harrison pay for the way he had hurt me. After that was accomplished, I planned never to see her again.

Roxie pulled a cigarette out of a pack, tapped it, and then stuck it in her mouth. She had never been allowed to smoke at Grandma's house and I wondered when she had picked up the habit. She lit it and took a long deep breath, her eyes squinted the whole time like she was deep in thought.

She finally said, "Christine said you're his personal assistant or something?"

"Executive assistant," I hissed.

She waved a wisp of smoke away from her face. "Yes, whatever. So you work closely with him at that prestigious law firm of his? You know the daily ins and outs of his work schedule, colleagues, cases, all that stuff?"

I nodded impatiently. "Yes, of course. That's what executive assistants do." Her snide "whatever" had stung a little.

"Good." A broad smile spread across her face. "Very good."

I frowned. "Good? What does that mean?"

"Nothing. Just let me take care of all this, hear? The less you know the better."

I stood there with a confused look on my face. Roxie disappeared into another room and came back with a legal pad and a pen. She sat down on the couch and motioned for me to sit down next to her. "I need some very specific information. I want you to think hard and give it to me clear, okay?"

I nodded, still not sure of what she had in mind. For the next thirty minutes, she grilled me on details of our workplace, Blake's schedule, different people who worked in the office. I gave her all the information she asked for, including my contact information. It didn't matter that she had my cell number since I would be getting a new phone with a new number when our dealings were done. And my office number wouldn't matter because I wouldn't be working for Blake anymore. After this was all over, she'd have no way of getting in touch with me.

She finally laid the pad and the pen down. "That should just about do it. If I think of anything else, I'll contact you."

"What am I supposed to do now?"

"Nothing. Absolutely nothing. Go home; get some good sleep to get rid of those dreadful bags under your eyes. Go to church tomorrow and repent for almost cutting your fiancé and your poor mother . . ." She chuckled and I gave her a look that could kill. "And then go to work Monday morning like this weekend never happened."

"Work? I can't go to work Monday. I don't ever want to see Blake Harrison again."

Roxie smiled and gently laid a hand on my arm. "Oh, but you can and you must. You have to become the world's best actress because he can't suspect anything's wrong between the two of you. You have to work like you've always worked and pretend like you still love him and think he's the most amazing thing that ever lived."

A sad look crossed into Roxie's eyes as she stared at my face. Last thing I needed was her feeling sorry for me because I got my heart broken. I stood and walked to her door.

"I'll try as hard as I can. It's hard to pretend you love somebody when you really want to stab them in the throat."

Roxie chuckled. "Just give me a couple of weeks. I promise it will be well worth it."

I gave her one last look, trying to figure out whether I should believe her. What if she was just another woman trying to get rid of me so she could have Blake to herself? What if this was all a scam she and Christine set up to make me lose the best thing that ever happened to me?

"Sabrina, I know I've never given you any reason to trust me. But trust me on this." The evil twinkle in Roxie's eyes made me shiver. "By the time I'm finished with Blake Harrison, he won't be hurting any mother's pretty little daughter. Ever again."

Chapter Six

I spent the rest of the weekend in bed, crying and sleeping. I couldn't bring myself to go to church. Monday morning, I got up and got myself dressed for work like I always did. I couldn't imagine how I could possibly make it through the day without Blake suspecting that I knew what I knew. How was I supposed to act like I still loved him? Follow his orders like I actually respected him? Be peaceful and calm like I hadn't thought of at least a hundred ways to murder him?

I arrived right at 8:00 A.M., the time I was paid to arrive at work but an hour later than when I usually got there. I had barely put my purse in my file drawer when Blake barged out of his office.

"Where have you been?" He looked down at his watch. "I've been waiting for you."

I pulled out my lunch bag and put it into the small refrigerator behind my desk. "What are you talking about? It's eight o'clock. I'm here." I batted my eyelashes a few times.

"Sabrina, you knew we needed to go over the Foster deposition first thing this morning and that I also needed the Connor files sent out. And you show up at . . . ." Blake must have noticed a few heads from neighboring offices turning in our direction. "Sabrina, can I see you in my office, please?"

I could tell it took everything in him not to slam the door behind me. "You knew we had things to take care of this morning and you come traipsing in here late like you don't even care. I hope you haven't let Friday night go to your head. You still work for me and I still expect you to do your job." He started shuffling papers around on his desk and muttered under his breath. "I knew I shouldn't have given you that ring until I made partner."

I clenched my teeth real tight and made myself take a couple of deep breaths.

He lowered his voice. "And where were you all weekend? I've been calling and texting you since Saturday evening and you haven't answered at all. Where have you been?"

The anger in his voice sent a chill up my spine. I had seen this side of him when things didn't go his way with a case or when he felt like someone was disrespecting him in the office, but it had never been directed at me. At least not this bad.

I looked down at the ground. "I was sick all weekend. Still not feeling well today really."

"So sick that you couldn't answer my phone calls?"

"My phone broke over the weekend. I didn't feel well enough to go out to get a new one." It wasn't like I was lying. My phone did break. And I was sick. So sick of him and his lies. And he knew I opted for a cell phone only instead of having a land line, so that wasn't an option.

"You didn't think to call me?"

I frowned. "We never talk on weekends, Blake. You're either traveling or . . . busy." I had a sour taste in my mouth just thinking about it.

He frowned as if he was trying to figure out if that was true. He finally came over and put his hands on my shoulders. "Well, of course that's going to change. After all, we are engaged, right?"

I bit my lip and nodded. Christine must have broken it off with him for good, so now he figured his weekends would be free. I wanted to rip his head off. I pulled away from him. "Right. I'll go ahead and get those files off and the deposition notes printed. Don't you have a meeting?"

"Do I?"

I walked over to his desk and grabbed the files I knew he would need for the meeting. I placed them in his hands and pushed him toward the door. "Yes. You need to review these files and you have a new client who'll be in the conference room in twenty minutes."

He gave me that admiring look that now made my stomach turn. "What would I do without you?"

I adjusted his tie and patted his shoulder. "I don't know, Blakey. I just don't know."

It was true. I didn't know how Blake functioned before I came into his life. I kept his schedule completely organized, both personally and professionally. Made sure his dry cleaning was done and delivered. Bought and mailed both his sisters' birthday and Christmas presents. I did the grocery shopping for his cook to make sure she had all his favorite foods. And once a month, I baked his favorite German chocolate cake that, according to him, tasted better than his mama's.

I had made myself completely indispensable as a personal assistant, and had presented myself as a perfect candidate for the perfect wife.

Or so I thought.

I walked back out to my desk and slowly sat down. I thought of all those faces in all those pictures. Everything I had done wasn't enough. He was just using me. To make partner and to keep his life in perfect order. How could I have thought that he loved me? I ran to the bathroom before the tears started falling down my face.

I went into the last stall and locked the door behind me so I could think for a minute. Why had he bothered to propose? I was giving him everything he wanted and needed without any promise of anything in return.

Well . . . almost everything. *Did he propose because I said I wouldn't have sex with him without a ring?* I remembered how angry he got when I said he couldn't come upstairs the night of our proposal. *So he just bought me a ring so he could have sex with me?* Seemed like a high price to pay when he was getting it free from so many other places.

I thought about talk shows I had seen where they talked about how men enjoyed the hunt. They would do whatever it took to get a woman in bed and then, afterward, they had no use for her. And the more a woman held out, the more they wanted her. Was that all I was to Blake? A challenge?

The more I thought about it, the sicker I felt. There was no way I could work the rest of the day. I came out of the bathroom stall and washed and dried my face. When I got back to my desk, I jotted Blake a brief note saying that, just as I had explained, I still wasn't feeling well and needed to go home. He would have a fit when he found out. He might as well get used to me not being around to make sure his life ran smoothly.

On the way home, I had to resist the urge to call Janine. I missed my best friend so much and really needed to talk to her. But it would be terrible to call her after dropping her for Blake now that it was clear Blake and I wouldn't be together. I thought of all my friends I had dropped for Blake. I wondered what it would be like to try to go back with my tail tucked between my legs now that everything they had said about him had proved to be true. There was no way I could do that. I would just have to depend on God to get me through this.

And I'd have to depend on Roxie to get revenge. And boy would she. I thought of the boyfriends who had pissed her off when we were growing up in Grandma's house together like sisters rather than mother and daughter. When they said that hell hath no fury like a woman scorned, they were talking about Roxie. A pot of boiling hot grits was child's play in her book. Her revenge was diabolical. For a minute, I almost felt sorry for Blake.

'Cause he was about to get it.

Chapter Seven

It had been over a week and still nothing from Roxie. No phone calls, e-mail, or signs of anything that would make Blake Harrison die a slow, painful death. Roxie had done it to me again. Made a bunch of promises that she had no plans of keeping. And I had fallen for it. Again.

The one thing Roxie had done for me was to keep me from doing something crazy and dangerous the day I had those knives in my purse. Maybe that was all God wanted it to be. To keep me from messing up my future. Not that I had much of a future without a man like Blake Harrison in my life.

Over the course of the week, my anger had dulled down to a numb pain. I no longer wanted to cut Blake. It was time to decide what to do next. I had been doing a pretty good job all week of faking like nothing was wrong, but it was getting played.

On the one hand, I was tired of pretending that everything was okay between me and him. On the other hand, it would be stupid for me to up and quit when I didn't have a new job to go to. I had started combing the want ads and submitted my resume a couple of places online. If things stayed quiet, I would wait things out here until I found a new job. How long would that be, though? I didn't have a college degree, and there were people out there with master's degrees who couldn't find a job.

My intercom beeped and Blake asked me to step into his office. When I walked in, he gestured for me to close the door. I stood at the door, waiting to see what he wanted.

"Sabrina, honey, I seem to have a kink in my shoulder. Can you try to work it out for me?" He turned his chair backward and pointed to his upper back.

Really? Does he really expect me to give him a massage right now? I imagined myself putting my hands on him, but not on his shoulders. I wanted to squeeze his neck until he stopped breathing. When I didn't come over to his desk, he turned around and looked at me. "Sabrina? What's wrong?"

"Nothing . . . I . . ." I folded my arms. "It's just that Harvin's secretary said something the other day that bothered me. She asked what you and I did behind closed doors all the time." It was a bald-faced lie and God would have to forgive me. I needed a good excuse for not having to touch Blake ever again.

Blake's eyes grew wide. "What?" He stood up and walked over to me. "What did she say? Who's talking about us?"

"Nobody's talking about us. Melissa just pulled me aside and mentioned it. Promised to keep it to herself."

"Keep it to herself? Keep what to herself? What does she think she knows about us?"

"Nothing, Blakey." I was enjoying seeing him nervous at the thought that someone might find out his little secret and that it could affect his chance of making partner. "I mean, Mr. Harrison." I couldn't help but smile.

"You think this is funny, Sabrina? It's not funny. You have to be more careful."

"I have to be more careful?" I put a hand on my hip. "What do you mean I have to be more careful? You're the one who called me in here for a massage."

"It's the way you look at me and talk to me. Anyone can tell that you have feelings for me. You walk around here like a lovesick puppy. You just have to do a better job of hiding it."

I started to feel last week's anger rise up in me. "Better job of hiding it?"

"Yes, Sabrina." He paced back to his desk and back to me again. "You cannot cost me this promotion."

"Cost you this promotion? What's that supposed to mean?"

He walked past me to open the door. "Nothing. Just . . . go on back to your desk and if I need anything, I'll let you know."

I walked back out to my desk, clenching my teeth.

A few seconds later, my intercom buzzed. I picked up my phone. "Yes, Mr. Harrison?"

"Ms. Rogers. I need you to make some reservations to New York this weekend. I have a client to meet with first thing Saturday morning. Go ahead and make the reservations for Friday night through Sunday afternoon. I'll take the train."

I couldn't speak.

"Sabrina?"

"I'm sorry. Client's name please?"

"Huh? Client's name? Wha . . . wha . . . do you . . ."

"The name of the client you'll be meeting with this weekend in New York?"

"That's not important," he barked. "Just make the reservation, Ms. Rogers."

I could hear him slam down the phone. I felt like slamming my own but there were too many eyes around. I was sure there was steam coming out of my ears. There was no way I was going to let him make a fool out of me again. I wasn't about to make reservations for him to go see his New York model mistress this weekend.

It was time for me to give him a piece of my mind. I pictured myself walking into his office, cussing him out, and creating a scene so loud that he did actually have to worry that I was going to cost him his promotion.

I suddenly had the urge to stab him again but the only knife I had was the plastic one in my lunch bag.

My intercom buzzed again. "Yes, Mr. Harrison?"

"Could you get me the nicest suite at the Grand Hotel? I need to have an . . . extra relaxing weekend."

That was it. *Forget waiting for a new job.* I stood and marched myself right into Blake's office. I slammed the door behind me and put my hands on my hips.

"Sabrina, what are you doing? Didn't we just decide that—"

Just as I was about to cuss him within an inch of his life—Roxie style—the door slammed open. I turned around to see what was going on. Lila Strauss, one of the other attorneys, stood there, bright red with such an angry look on her face that I was scared.

"Mr. Harrison, what the hell is this?" She threw a brown box wrapped with a large pink bow onto his desk.

Blake looked from her to me and then down at the box. "What? What is it?"

"It was just delivered with a card from you that read, 'Hope this fulfills all your needs.' Is this some kind of sick joke?"

"I have no idea what you're talking about."

"Take a look."

Blake picked up the box and peered inside. His eyes widened and his mouth fell open. "I didn't do this. I wouldn't do anything like this."

Before he could get the words out, Kara Hopkins, another attorney, stormed in. She slammed the door behind her. "How dare you! I never . . ." She threw another brown box onto the desk next to the first one. "For all my lonely nights? How dare you!"

All the color drained from Blake's face. "I didn't—"

The door slammed open again. "I have never been so insulted in all my life!" West's executive assistant burst into the office and joined the impromptu party. Margaret Slaughter was an older lady, in her early fifties or so. "'Just in case he can't anymore?' Mr. Harrison, I hope you have a good explanation for this."

Blake came from behind his desk. "Ladies, I assure you, I didn't send these boxes. Please, give me a little while to get to the bottom of this. You can't possibly think I would have done anything like this." He laid a hand on Lila's and Kara's shoulders. "Please, I'll have an explanation for you before the afternoon is out."

This seemed to calm them down. He walked them out of his office, speaking quietly to avoid a further stir. He turned back toward me and said over his shoulder with pleading eyes, "Ms. Rogers, could you dispose of these for me, please?"

I nodded, anxious to see what was in the boxes that had caused such an uproar. I picked up the card on one of the boxes. My mouth fell open when I saw that they had been sent from Izzy's Sex Shoppe.

I peered out Blake's door to see if anyone was watching. I couldn't stop myself from looking into the box. I turned bright red when I saw the contents and dropped the box on the floor.

"Sabrina! I thought I asked you to dispose of those." Blake stormed back into the office.

I grabbed the trash can and swept the two boxes off Blake's desk into it. "Sorry, Mr. Harrison." I leaned over to pick up the other box and threw it into the can.

Oh my God. . . . I covered my mouth with my hand. I can't believe she would . . .

"Sabrina . . ." Blake was visibly shaken. "I mean Ms. Rogers. Can you please get me the phone number for this . . . store so I can figure out how this could have possibly happened?"

I leaned over the trash can, pulled one of the cards off the top box, and passed it to Blake.

He narrowed his eyes. "I didn't mean . . . Never mind."

I walked out of his office and closed the door behind me.

Before I could sit down at my desk, Paris came sauntering up with a huge smile on her face. She had that Cheshire cat grin she always had when she had some juicy gossip she couldn't hold on to.

She held out a thick stack of papers. "Your mail." She stood there.

"Thanks, Paris." I sat down at my desk, hoping she would go away so I could try to overhear Blake's conversation with the sex shop people.

She didn't move. "Aren't you gonna look at it?"

"Huh?" I frowned.

"Look at Mr. Harrison's mail." She looked like she was about to bust with excitement.

I looked down at the stack of mail I had plopped onto my desk. I tossed aside a couple of interoffice mail envelopes and advertising brochures for upcoming law conferences. And then I saw what Paris was so excited about.

My mouth dropped open. In my hand were two magazines. On the front cover of the first one was a man who was almost completely naked, with thick black eyeliner and a half smile on his face. I looked at the name of the magazine—*Out*. I gasped. The other magazine, *Unzipped*, had two half-naked men hugging each other on the cover. Each magazine had an address label on the front with Blake's name and the office address. *Roxie subscribed Blake to gay magazines?*

I looked up at Paris and back down at the magazines, unable to close my mouth. "Where did you get these?"

"They came in the mail this morning. I wanted to deliver them myself to keep things discreet. I wouldn't want just anybody to see them. You know some people can't hold water." She gave a little wave and a giggle and walked off.

Blake's office door flew open. "They're saying that the order was placed online using my credit card. They had my name, address, and all my credit card information. How could this have happened?"

I was still sitting there with the magazines in my hand, with my mouth open.

"Sabrina, are you listening to me?" When I still didn't move, Blake snatched the magazines out of my hand. He frowned as he studied the cover models and title of each one. He turned bright red when his eyes drifted to the address label. "What in the . . ."

He looked down at the magazines and up at me. "Where did you get these?"

I flinched. "Paris just brought them up from the mail room."

His eyes bugged out. "Paris?"

I nodded, bracing myself for his outburst. To my surprise, he simply turned around, walked back into his office, and slammed the door.

I held my head in my hands for a second, unable to believe everything that had just happened. My brand new cell phone chimed to let me know I had gotten a text. I peered down at the screen and almost fell out of my chair when I read:

Sometimes a woman just has to let a man know. This is only the beginning. Welcome to Roxie's Ten Steps to Revenge.

Chapter Eight

The next evening at around eight, my cell phone rang. I saw Blake's number and automatically went through a mental checklist. His dry cleaning was delivered yesterday. I had given him a copy of his updated schedule before I left work. His refrigerator and pantry were well stocked. I wasn't sure why he was calling but I didn't feel like being bothered by him at the moment.

The phone chimed to indicate that he'd left a voice mail. I didn't even care to listen to it. A few seconds later, a different chime came through for a text. I still didn't move from the bed. I had spent most evenings in the bed since I had found out the truth about Blake. The evenings were too long to be depressed and brokenhearted, wondering about a new job and downsizing my apartment. It was easier just to sleep.

The phone rang again and then stopped and then rang again. *Whatever it is must be urgent.* I was about to continue to ignore it, but then remembered Roxie's ten steps and thought Blake might be suffering from the next step. Excitement rose up in my heart as I tried to imagine what Roxie had done.

"Hello?"

"Sabrina, why aren't you answering my phone calls? I'm in the middle of an emergency. It shouldn't take this long to get in touch with you."

I couldn't help but smile. "Sorry, Blakey, I was in the middle of something. What's wrong?"

"I need you to come right this minute and bring me a credit card. Drive as fast as you can."

"What's wrong, Blake?"

"This is not the time to ask a million questions." His voice went low and tight and I knew he was trying to mask his anger from whoever he was with. "Just get here and bring your credit card."

I closed my eyes and pulled up a mental picture of his calendar. I realized he was at a potential client dinner with the bigwigs of the Peterson Corporation. *Oh, this is serious . . .*

"Well, how much is it? I'm not sure I can afford to pay for—"

"Sabrina, obviously I'm going to pay you back." I knew he was doing all he could not to scream at me. "Just get here. Call me when you're in the lobby." He hung up on me.

I laughed to myself and slipped into the suit I'd worn that day and headed for my car.

Knowing his calendar by heart, I headed to the restaurant I knew he was dining at. When I arrived, I called Blake from the lobby. He had that harried, stressed-out look on his face he got the few times he had lost a case. He held out his hand for my card.

"Blake, how much is it? I don't know if I have enough money in my account to cover the cost of a dinner here."

He frowned as he pulled the card out of my hand. "How could you not have four hundred dollars in your account? Are you that financially irresponsible?"

I bit my lip to keep from mentioning that growing up dirt poor made me the kind of person who always kept a large amount of money in my savings account. I kept the bare minimum in my checking account so that every spare cent could be collecting interest. In that moment, I realized how very little Blake knew about me.

"Financially irresponsible? I'm not the one borrowing my assistant's credit card to pay for a client's dinner."

"It's not that I don't have the money, Sabrina." His face contorted into an angry glare. "There's something wrong with my credit cards. Both business and personal. I don't know what the problem is, but for now, I need to pay this bill."

"Of course, Blake. I'll be waiting in my car for the card." I turned on my heel and walked out the front door. I kept my smile hidden until I got to my car. I sat there for a few minutes, enjoying the thought of how embarrassed Blake must have been when they ran both his credit cards and brought the bill back to the table still unpaid. I could only imagine what kind of excuses he had come up with to save his reputation.

I sat in my car, watching the door, waiting for Blake and his clients to emerge, but a large tow truck pulled into the parking lot, obstructing my view. It paused there for a second and finally moved. After a few moments, it maneuvered its way around the parking lot and stopped in front of Blake's car. My eyes flew open when the driver got out and started attaching his rig to the Mercedes. *What has Roxie done now?*

After a few minutes, Blake emerged from the restaurant with three men in expensive-looking suits, talking confidently with his usual hand gestures. I followed his eyes as they traveled to his car and saw it being attached to the tow truck.

He stopped mid-conversation and ran over to the driver. "What on earth are you doing to my car?"

I rolled down my windows so I could hear, although knowing Blake, things would soon get loud enough that I'd be able to hear with the windows closed.

"Your car is being repossessed for nonpayment, sir."

"What?" I could hear Blake's voice go up three octaves. "Nonpayment? That's ridiculous!" Blake nervously eyed his potential clients and then turned his attention back to the driver. "There's been some mistake. You must have the wrong car."

The driver pulled out his clipboard and said, "Are you Mr. Blake Harrison of 1487 Sixteenth Street, Washington, DC?"

Blake's eyes widened. "I am, but—"

"Then there's no mistake. This is the vehicle I'm supposed to take." The driver dismissed Blake and continued hooking up his rig.

I could tell Blake didn't know whether he should try to clear things with the clients or argue with the tow truck driver. He turned to the men, undoubtedly trying to explain to them that this was a huge mistake. He shook each of their hands and gave them one of his cards. By the time he finished schmoozing and the potential clients left, the tow truck driver had finished hooking his car up and had climbed into the cab.

"Can you please tell me where you got your information? What is the name of your company?"

The driver ignored him and started up his truck.

Blake began to yell. "You have no idea who you're dealing with. I will sue your company and you'll never work again, do you hear me?"

The driver shrugged and slowly pulled out of the parking lot.

Blake stood there for a few minutes, watching his S-Class being pulled down the street. I got out of the car in time to hear him curse loudly.

"Oh, Blake! I'm so sorry. Can I take you home?" It was hard to be all fake and pretend I cared. It was even harder to realize that he didn't see through my bad acting. Did this man really pay me any attention at all? Had he ever?

He slowly walked over to the car. I decided to pour it on thick. I ran around and opened the car door for him. It would probably kill him to get into my Corolla. I tried to ignore the disgusted look on his face as he surveyed the interior of my car.

"I'm so sorry, sweetie," I said. "I know that must have been embarrassing. First the credit card and then the car. Is everything okay? Is there something we need to talk about?"

"No, there's nothing we need to talk about." His voice burst with raw anger.

"Blake, there is absolutely no reason to yell at me. I'm trying to help you, remember?"

"You don't have to remind me. And I don't need your help."

I held out my hand.

"What?" he barked.

"My credit card. I don't want you to forget to give it to me. Will you have enough money to pay me back?"

His eyes shot daggers at me. "Sabrina, I'm not broke."

We sat in silence for a few minutes with him sulking and me doing everything in my power not to laugh at how pitiful he looked.

I finally reached over and stroked his hair and then moved down to massage his shoulder. It took awhile, but he relaxed after a few minutes.

"Sorry for yelling at you. None of this was your fault. It doesn't make any sense. First the credit cards and then my car. It's all so ridiculous."

I continued massaging his shoulder. "It's okay, honey. I'm sure that was upsetting for you."

"I needed that account. I don't understand what's going on. It's like someone is out to get me. Trying to sabotage me from making partner. I wonder if it's someone in the company." He sat there brooding for a second. "I bet it's Lila Strauss. She probably sent hers and the other two packages to make me look bad. She probably ordered the subscriptions to those . . . disgusting magazines." He stroked his chin, deep in thought. "You think she's trying to sabotage me so she can make partner? I bet that's it. Well, if she thinks she can get away with this, she's in for a rude awakening."

"She wouldn't do that, Blake. Tamper with your credit cards and personal financial information? That's illegal. She wouldn't go that far."

"Then who else could it be? Who else would do these types of things to me? I'm a good, hardworking person who treats everyone honest and fair. Why would anyone want to destroy me?"

"I can't imagine, honey," I said sweetly. "I just can't imagine."

We rode in silence the rest of the way back to his building. When we got to the front door, he placed his hand on the door handle to get out and then froze. He looked at me and then at the front of his building and then back at me again.

"What's wrong?"

"Nothing. I . . . Can you take me around back, through the garage?"

"What? Why?"

"Sabrina, please. Not a million questions. I've had a horrible day. A horrible week, really. Can you take me through the back?"

I leaned past him to look at the front door to see what had made him so jumpy. There stood Roxie chatting with the doorman. It was all I could do not to laugh as Blake nervously turned his entire body in my direction and held a hand up to cover the side of his face. "Sabrina, please. I just want to get inside and rest."

It was time to make him really suffer. I took a deep breath and used a trick Roxie had taught me as a child when we were trying to get something over on my grandmother. I burst into tears.

Blake's eyes widened. "What is wrong with you?"

"Why are you so ashamed of me? You asked me to marry you, but you're embarrassed to be seen with me."

Blake turned to the front of the building to see what Roxie was doing. She looked like she was having the most interesting conversation with the doorman—like she didn't plan on being finished anytime soon.

"Ashamed of you? What are you—"

"I always have to go up the back elevator. You take me hours away to another city to go out to dinner. You bought me that beautiful ring and I can't even wear it. And now you're embarrassed to be seen getting out of my car in front of your building. How can I marry you and you can't even be seen with me in public?"

I covered my face with my hands and let my shoulders shake dramatically, letting out deep sobbing sounds. "Do you even love me?"

Blake cursed under his breath. "I can't believe this." He put a hand on my shoulder. "Of course I do. That ring should prove it. The very fact that I'm willing to risk my career and everything to be with you should prove it."

I uncovered my face. "You love me? You're not ashamed of me?"

"Of course I'm not ashamed of you." He looked at the front of the building again and back at me. I enjoyed watching him squirm at the dilemma I had created.

He couldn't ask me to drive around to the back of the building after my outburst. But he also couldn't get out of the car with Roxie still standing there with the doorman.

He said, "Okay, here's the truth. That woman in the door there . . . she's this lonely old cougar who's always hounding me. I was nice enough to hold the elevator for her one day and she took it as an invitation to sleep with her. So I avoid her as much as possible. I asked you to take me around back so I wouldn't have to run into her."

Blake put a hand on my face. "See, I'm not ashamed of you at all. You know how I feel about you, Sabrina."

I refused to let him get away with the lie. "This is the perfect way to get rid of her then. If she knows you're with someone, she'll leave you alone."

He raised his eyebrows. "You don't know women like that. They're desperate. It'll only make her chase me harder."

"No, it won't. You'll see." I opened my car door to get out. I knew the doorman would come running. He turned from Roxie and spotted Blake in my front seat. He quickstepped down the walk to get Blake's door. Roxie didn't leave her post at the front of the building, only yards away from us. Blake looked horrified. I walked around to his side of the car after the doorman let him out.

"I love you, Blake." I threw my arms around his neck and planted a big kiss on his lips. I thought he would die.

I guessed Roxie decided to let him off easy because when the kiss was over, she had disappeared. Blake was visibly relieved. He put his arms around me. "Thanks for coming to get me tonight, honey. I do appreciate you." He looked at the front door of his building and then back at me. "I know things between us aren't ideal, but soon everything will be different. You'll see."

"I know. Sorry I got so upset. I . . . love you so much. I just want us to be together and everything to be normal." I almost puked saying that I loved him.

He kissed me on the nose and took one last glance at the front of his building. "I know, dear. They will be." He walked around to my side of the car and opened the door for me to get in. He leaned into the window and kissed me. "Thanks again. I don't know what I'd do without you."

You'll soon find out. I gave him a syrupy-sweet smile and drove off. As soon as I was out of his sight, I wiped the back of my hand across my lips.

A few moments later, my cell phone vibrated. I looked at the screen and saw a text message from Roxie:

> Did you see his face when he saw me? I thought he would pee in his pants! Can't wait to hear what the tears were all about. Drive down the block, wait five minutes, then come back and see me. We need to plot out the next steps in our plan.

Chapter Nine

I made my usual trip up the service elevator to the tenth floor where Roxie lived. I walked down the long hall quickly, watching to make sure the coast was clear as I approached her condo and knocked. When I did, Roxie pulled me inside quickly and closed the door and leaned against it. A broad grin spread across her face. "Now that was the most fun I've had in a looonng time."

We both laughed and I followed her into her living room.

"You have to tell me everything! I trust the packages and the magazines arrived as ordered?"

We both howled with laughter as I explained the scene in the office she had created with her packages from Izzy's.

She wiped her eyes and leaned back against the couch. "And I was right to guess that you'd be the person bringing him home tonight. I knew he'd be too embarrassed to let anyone else know his car got repossessed."

"How in the world did you do that?"

Roxie held up a finger and shook her head. "Ah ah ah. Remember the rule. The less you know, the better. You let your mama handle the bad stuff."

"Did you see him sweating in my front seat when we pulled up? That was so perfect."

Roxie said, "The tow truck driver called when he pulled off so I was able to guess what time to plant myself downstairs. Now what were all those tears about?"

I told her about Blake's wanting to be dropped off in the garage. Her eyes went wide and she burst into laughter. "You really wanted to make him suffer, huh? I'm gonna make him suffer for calling me a desperate, lonely old cougar. He might get twenty steps for that."

We both laughed. Roxie looked me in the eyes and her voice went soft. "How are you doing with all of this? I know it hasn't been easy, still being around him and all. You okay?"

"I'm fine." I looked away from her. I hated seeing the care and concern in her eyes. I didn't want her thinking we were going to have any relationship when this was all over. "So what's next? What information do you need?"

She stared at my face for a second, with that guilty, regretful look. "Did you love him, Sabrina?"

I rolled my eyes. "Roxie, I'm here because you said we needed to plan out the next step. If I had known you wanted to have a mother-daughter chat, I would have gone on home."

"I just want to make sure you're okay before we go on."

"I said I was fine." The words came out mean and venomous. I didn't care. She deserved it.

She sat there quiet for a few seconds. "Is it a crime for me to ask about your feelings? You were engaged to this man and now we're destroying his life. Before we plot out the next step, I was—"

"Spare me. It's too late for you to be worried about my feelings now. Were you thinking about my feelings when you left me twelve years ago? I mean, now all of a sudden you want to be my mother and care about what I'm going through? Where were you when I got my first period? Had my first kiss? Went to the prom? Was trying to figure out what college I was going to? Where were you when Grandma died?"

Roxie's eyes widened. "I was there when she died."

My mouth flew open. "You came to the funeral and sat in the back and left after you viewed her body. You didn't say even a word to me. Just rushed out the back door."

Roxie's head dropped.

"Where were you when I was trying to figure out how I was going to live without her? When I had to drop out of college and get a job because I couldn't afford to stay in school without her support? It's too late to care, Roxie."

She sat there, deflated. "So you're gonna hate me forever?"

I let out a deep breath. "Do you want more information about Blake or should I go?"

She rose from the couch and disappeared into one of her bedrooms. A few moments later, she returned with her legal pad.

Without making eye contact, I laid out Blake's schedule for the week in great detail. Normally I would have been proud to know his schedule and plans so well. Now I felt like a stupid idiot, completely lost in the life of a man who could not care less about me.

"He has a huge presentation next Saturday morning. You throw a monkey wrench in that and he's doomed." I smiled at the thought of what she would dream up and what it would do to Blake.

Roxie laughed. "Hmmm . . . I guess you got some of your mama's devilment in you, huh?"

The smile left my face. "No. I'm not anything like you."

She smirked. "Really? You're more like me than you want to believe. More than you want to be."

"How so? You don't know anything about me so how can you say that? I'm not like you at all."

"No?" She leaned in close to me and stared me straight in the eye. "Then why were you going to marry Blake?"

I pulled back from her. "What?"

"Why were you going to marry Blake Harrison? I asked you before, did you love him? Or was he just a way up in the world?"

I opened my mouth to protest and then stopped. *Was I marrying Blake because of his money? His social status?*

"You judge me for marrying Mr. St. James for money, but yet you were planning to do the very same thing. You don't love that man, Sabrina. How could you? He's as mean as a snake and only cares about himself. But he could rescue you from struggling and living the poor life. You could move into the penthouse, get a new wardrobe, a new car, everything you ever dreamed of. Isn't that how it works?"

I just stared at her.

"See, Sabrina. You are just like me."

I wanted to scratch her eyeballs out. "There's a big difference. I didn't leave a little girl behind like you did."

"Didn't you though? Look at you. You don't have any friends, no life, everything centers around Blake. You did leave a little girl behind. You."

Her words slammed into my chest.

Her cell phone let out a short jazzy tune. She rose to pick it up from the end table and smirked when she looked at the screen. "Just as I thought. After the little show you put on downstairs, Mr. Harrison knows he's got some serious making up to do. I need to get upstairs."

I rose and walked slowly to the door, still reeling from the words she had said to me.

Roxie followed me to the door. "Sabrina, there's nothing I can do to make up for what I did. I would give anything to go back and change that decision. If I had it to do all over again, I would have stayed poor and broke just to see my little girl grow up. And maybe if I had been there, you wouldn't be making the same wrong decisions and choices I made. All I want is for you to forgive me and give me a chance to be in your life again."

I reached out for the doorknob. "If you need any more information on Blake, send me a text or an e-mail. Hopefully, you have all you need to finish your ten steps."

I opened the door. "Good-bye, Roxie."

As I closed the door behind me, I tried not to see the tears trickling down both her cheeks.

Chapter Ten

The next morning I woke up and arranged a car service for Blake to get to work. I knew there was no way he would want me driving him to work in my car. Roxie made the necessary calls to get his car released and I arranged to have it towed to the office so Blake could drive himself home. Roxie did whatever she had to do to fix Blake's credit card situation and all was well in his world again. At least until Roxie unleashed the next step in her plan.

Blake spent the entire morning thanking me and then slipped me some money to take the rest of the day off to go to the spa. I decided to put the $400 he returned and the extra money in the bank. I needed to save as much as I could. I could rest at home rather than at the spa.

As I was driving home, my phone rang. I thought it was Blake, realizing he needed me back at the office. When I looked down at the caller ID, Janine's number was flashing on the screen. It was her weekly call.

I paused for a second and decided to answer it. "Hello?"

"Sabrina, I can't believe you answered the phone. How are you? It's Janine."

"I know who this is, silly. I'm . . . fine. Ummm, how are you?" I got out of the car and started up the walk to my apartment.

"I'm fine. Wow, I can't believe I'm actually talking to you. Thanks for answering. It must be God. The past couple of weeks you've been on my mind a lot. I've been praying for you. Everything okay?"

I stared at the phone, not knowing what to say. "Sure. Everything's fine."

Janine laughed. "I know we haven't talked in months but I still know you. You're not fine. What's going on?"

My silence for the next few seconds messed up any chance I had of convincing Janine that I was okay. She was one of those people who could see straight through a person, so lying wouldn't do me any good. I decided to give it a try because telling the truth about my messy life was too embarrassing. "Work is stressful right now. That's all. Blake is up for partner and we're both working really hard. I had to take the afternoon off to recover."

"So things are still good between the two of you?"

I couldn't dance around a direct question like that. As I sat there trying to think of a lie to tell her, she said, "I made your favorite—chicken and dumplings—almost as good as your grandmother's. You remember where I live?"

"Janine, I—"

"I'm not taking no for an answer, Sabrina. I won't have any peace until I know what's wrong with you. Don't you think God put you on my heart for a reason?"

"I really appreciate you and God being concerned about me, but I really need some rest."

"Okay, I'll be over there, then. See you in about thirty minutes. You still live in the same place, right?

"Janine . . ."

"Come on, Brina. Don't you want to see your best friend?"

I almost started crying when she said those words. "You still consider me your best friend?"

"Always, girl. And I'm about to perform one of the most important best friend duties: being there when things go wrong with your man. Should I bring gummy bears?"

A few tears did stream down my face when she said that. "Yeah. Gummy bears. And Skittles, too."

Janine laughed. "Wow, that bad?"

I started crying full force into the phone.

"Oh, Brina. I'm sorry. Be there in a few."

Janine just sat there with her mouth open when I told her about Blake's proposal and then my meeting with Christine. When I got to the part about Roxie, she fell off the couch in her classic, dramatic Janine fashion. When I told her that I had gone to Blake's building with knives in my purse and ran into Roxie instead, she rolled on the floor, clutching her chest.

"Oh my God!" She stopped rolling and sat up and looked at me. "You saw her? You actually saw your mother? What did you say when you saw her? Does she look the same? Were you glad to see her? Oh my goodness, Brina, this is really big! God is so good! I can't believe He brought your mother back into your life."

I frowned at her. "God is so good? How you figure? I just lost my fiancé and found out that my long-lost mother was one of four women sleeping with him. Now, years after abandoning me when I needed her the most, she wants to be all up in my life again. What's good about that?"

Janine popped up off the floor and onto the couch next to me. She grabbed both of my hands. "I can't believe you. This is God and it's all good." She jumped up off the couch and started pacing the living room. "What do I always tell you? It's just a matter of perspective." She put her hands on her hips. "Have you talked to God about all this?"

I frowned and looked down at my feet.

"That's what I thought." She paced the floor again, frowning like she was thinking real hard.

Janine struggled to fill a size two and always complained about not being able to gain weight. I told her it was because she was a constant ball of motion. She couldn't sit on the couch and have a normal conversation like a normal person. She was up and down, pacing, no matter what we were talking about. Even if we were in a setting where she was forced to sit still, her arms were in motion and her mouth going a mile a minute.

"Janine, you're making me dizzy and tired. Sit down."

"Sorry." She plopped down onto the couch next to me. I knew it wouldn't last for long but at least I'd get a second to rest my nerves before she started moving again.

"All I'm saying is that you need to see this for the blessing that it is. God protected you from marrying Blake"—Janine rolled her eyes—"which would have been a disaster. And He brought your mother back. After all these years, you get to have a relationship with her."

I started to protest but that would have been a slap in the face to Janine. Her own mother had died when she was two, so the thought of having a mother and not wanting to be close to her was unimaginable to Janine.

"You have to see this as a blessing. Otherwise you're going to miss it. A chance to have a mommy."

I knew there was no way I could explain to her how much I hated Roxie and how I never planned to let her be a part of my life.

"So tell me about her. What's she like?"

Janine looked so excited it was hard not to tell her something about Roxie. "She looks like me. Add sixteen years and thirty pounds and you got Roxie."

She raised her eyebrows. "How come you call your mother by her first name?"

I let out a deep breath. I had never gone in depth with Janine about what had happened with Roxie leaving me. She so romanticized her thoughts and memories about her own mother that it seemed rude. Maybe I needed to tell her now. Otherwise, knowing Janine, she would drive me crazy wanting me and Roxie to have the perfect mother-daughter relationship. Maybe if she realized that Roxie wasn't mother material, she wouldn't force the issue.

"Roxie had me when she was sixteen. As I got older and she had her boyfriends around, she never wanted me to call her Mama because she was afraid I'd scare the men off. She let most of them believe I was her little sister."

Janine frowned.

"Yeah. She's a real piece of work." I told Janine the rest of the story—how Roxie left me for Mr. St. James and never sent any money even though she had plenty and knew me and Grandma were struggling. How she traveled the world and only bothered to send us a postcard from all the different places she got to see. How she walked away and never looked back. I figured Janine would agree with me that I was better off without her in my life.

"But she's different now, right? She wants to be in your life? She asked your forgiveness?"

I rolled my eyes and Janine jumped up and started pacing again. "You have to forgive her. Christians have to forgive."

Had it been that long since I had been to church? Why was Janine's mentioning God every other word and being all preachy getting on my last nerve? Had I backslidden that much in my five months of being gone?

"God forgave you and you have to forgive her."

Janine was one of those big-hearted people who was always talking about love and forgiveness. She did stuff like feed the homeless and also served in the prison ministry through our church. Even though her mother died when she was young, her father was well off and Janine still grew up with this perfect life, never wanting for anything. So it was easy for her to be all loving and forgiving all the time.

"Spare me the sermon, Janine. You have no idea what it's like to—"

"To what? Lose your mother and get her back? You're right. I have no idea."

I let out a deep breath and lay back on the couch with my eyes closed. There was no way I would be able to get her to see things my way. *I should have never let her come over.*

"I do know what it's like to be abandoned by someone you love for a man." Janine marched over to her huge purse and dug out the Skittles and gummy bears and dropped them in my lap. "And I love you and forgive you."

She plopped down on the couch next to me. Once again, I had to admit to myself that I was turning out to be more like Roxie than I wanted to be. How was it that I hated her so much and hated what she did to me, but I was making the same mistakes with my life?

"So now what?" Janine ripped open the bag of Skittles and popped a few in her mouth. There was no way I was going to tell her about teaming up with Roxie to get revenge on Blake. She'd never stop pacing and preaching.

I shrugged. "I don't know." I opened the Gummy Bears and pulled a red one apart. "I promise I'll pray about it, okay?"

Janine glared at me. "You're just saying that to get me off your back."

We both laughed.

"And what about Blake? What did he say when you confronted him?"

I closed my eyes and rubbed my temples. "I didn't confront him yet. I'm waiting until I find a new job."

She popped up off the couch and practically sprinted to the front door and back. "What?" She grabbed her head and shook it. "You haven't said anything? You find out that your fiancé is sleeping with four other women including your mother and you act like nothing happened? Are you crazy? How can you even do that?"

"It's complicated."

"You mean you can forgive a cheating, lying man, but you can't forgive your own mother? How is that possible?"

"I haven't forgiven him either. I . . ." How could I explain without explaining?

"What are you not telling me, Sabrina? What's really going on?"

I closed my eyes and put my head in my hands.

Janine sat down on the couch next to me. "What is it? Just tell me. It can't be that bad."

I sat there without saying anything.

She narrowed her eyes and put her hands on her hips. "Are you going to tell me or do I have to use my torture techniques?"

I reluctantly told her about Roxie's revenge. By the time I finished, Janine was laid out on the floor with her hand dramatically draped across her forehead, moaning.

"Are you crazy? I know Blake was wrong but don't you think that's a little extreme?"

"All that is Roxie's doing. I haven't done a thing."

"You have! You've given her all the information she needs to destroy his life. How can you do this?"

"A minute ago you were asking me how I could forgive him, now you're fussing at me for not forgiving him?"

"There's a difference between confronting the man and secretly plotting to ruin his life. This is bad, Sabrina. Really bad. You need to talk to God about this."

"Janine, I don't need you to preach to me. Just be my friend."

"I can't be your friend without telling you the truth. This is wrong and you need to stop."

I rose from the couch. "Thanks for being such a great friend. I promise I'll pray about it. Like I said when you called, I'm really tired. I appreciate you coming over. I promise we'll hang out again soon, okay?"

Janine followed me to the door. "Putting me out, huh? Okay. Don't think I'm gonna let you disappear like you did before. I see what happens when I leave you on your own for too long."

I laughed.

"Maybe I'll see you at church on Sunday? If God doesn't strike you down before then?"

I laughed again and allowed Janine to pull me into one of her fierce hugs. "Love you, Brina. Don't forget to talk to God so He can set you straight." She paused for a second. "Better yet, I'm gonna talk to God. And you know what that means."

I nodded and let her out the door. It meant that something was going to happen, soon. I guessed since Janine's heart was so perfect, God listened to her prayers more. Anytime she prayed about anything, she always got what she asked for.

Well, Janine would have to pray. I wasn't ready to talk to God yet. If I listened to Him for very long, He might talk some sense into me and tell me to forgive Roxie like she asked and let her into my life again. He would surely tell me to forgive Blake and that vengeance was His. And I wasn't trying to hear that.

The truth was I couldn't wait to see Roxie's next steps.

Chapter Eleven

On Sunday morning I turned over in bed and actually thought about going to church. Then I thought about my conversation with Janine on Friday and remembered I wasn't trying to hear what God might have to say, so I needed to stay away from His voice right now.

My cell phone chimed that a text message had come through. I picked it up and recognized Roxie's number.

Meet me at Meriwether Baptist Church for morning service. Come in late and sit in the balcony. Don't allow yourself to be seen.

Oh boy. That was Blake's church, which I had never been allowed to attend with him. What did Roxie have up her sleeve now?

I followed her instructions and snuck up to the balcony at 10:25 for the 10:00 A.M. service. I sat on an end row in the back. A few minutes later, I saw Roxie slip in at the opposite end of the balcony. She slid into a seat and took off her large sunglasses. She looked around until she saw me. She winked and gave me a small smile. I nodded and returned a small smile. Then I sat back in my seat and waited for the show to begin.

Thankfully, I had gotten there late enough to miss most of the boring service. Blake went to a sadity, upper-crusty church with absolutely no spirit whatsoever. All the rich, important people in DC went there, more to show off their fancy cars and clothes rather than to praise God. It was so stiff in there you better not clap your hands other than a polite pitty-pat after a song. And don't even think about saying "Hallelujah" or "Praise the Lord" out loud. Everyone would turn around and give you a look that let you know not to disrupt their service like that.

I sat through most of the boring sermon wondering what possible message anyone could have gotten out of it. The pastor had been talking for twenty minutes and I didn't see, hear, or feel Jesus in anything he said.

It seemed like his sermon was timed to end after exactly twenty-five minutes. The deacons stood across the front to give an altar call. I looked over at Roxie to see if I had missed something. Church was about to end and nothing had happened. She saw the question in my eyes and winked again and then smiled such an evil smile that I was afraid for Blake as to what was about to happen next.

A nice-looking family went up to the altar to join the church. And then I heard a loud wailing. The church went silent except for the organ playing "Come to Jesus." The wailing got louder as a woman with a blond weave approached the altar. She fell to her knees when she reached the front. One of the deacons reached to pat her on the back, and it seemed to make the wailing louder. He looked around for help and one of the church mothers came with a fan, as if flapping it wildly would calm whatever was wrong with this woman.

The pastor didn't seem to know what to do with such an emotional outburst in his church and kept his distance in the pulpit. The deacons looked to him to come restore the decorum to their stodgy service. The woman finally stood to her feet. "Thank you, Jesus. Thank you, Jesus."

She wore a red-hot dress that fit all her curves in all the right places and looked more appropriate for the club on Saturday night rather than church on Sunday morning. I looked closer and realized why she looked familiar.

She had our face. It was the Philly girl. *Oh dear.* What had Roxie done?

"Thank you, Jesus." She rocked and moaned. The deacon patted her shoulder, seeming relieved that she had chosen to calm down some. The pastor came down from the pulpit to the family who approached the altar and spoke quietly to them. He then turned to the congregation and said, "Meriwether Baptist Church, we have the Hunt family joining us on their Christian experience. Please give them a hand to welcome them."

He walked over to the Philly girl and spoke quietly to her. She had calmed herself down enough to have a conversation with him. Next thing you knew, she pulled the microphone out of his hand and said, "I need to thank Jesus and share my testimony." The pastor looked shocked. When he went to take the mic out of her hand, she stepped away a little and continued to address the crowd. "Saints, please pray for me. I found out some terrible news this week. I went to the doctor and found out that I was HIV positive."

A ripple of murmurs scattered across the congregation. The pastor looked too shocked to move.

Philly girl kept on talking. "I came here to confront the person who gave it to me. I really came to kill him. But during the service, the Lord touched my heart and I've been able to forgive." She lifted her arms in the air. "Blake Harrison, I forgive you for ruining my life. I forgive you for giving me this horrible disease. I came here to kill you but God has spared you. So now I forgive you. I forgive you." There was a loud stir in the congregation as the pastor finally succeeded in wrestling the microphone out of her hand.

She threw her hands in the air again and began moaning and rocking, "Thank you, Jesus. Thank you, Jesus."

I stared over at Roxie with my mouth open. She put her finger on her chin and gestured upward. I closed my mouth. I started to get up and leave but she held up a finger and shook her head slightly. I sat back down and followed her eyes to the lower level. A few minutes later, I saw Blake rise from the third pew, his long strides quickly taking him out of view.

A few minutes later, my phone vibrated. I looked down at the text on the screen. It was from Blake:

> Cancel all my appointments for tomorrow. I need to go to the doctor.

Minutes later, Roxie put on her sunglasses, held up five fingers, and exited down the back steps.

I sat there, unable to believe what had just happened. I counted in my head. Sex toys, gay magazines, credit cards, car repossessed. If this was only step five of ten in her revenge plan, I was scared for Blake at the thought of what might happen next.

Chapter Twelve

I sat in the balcony until I was sure both Blake and Roxie were gone. I hadn't felt God one bit during that dry, boring service, but I was sure feeling Him right now. The conviction was about to eat me up. Blake had done us all wrong—especially me and Christine—but he didn't deserve what we had just done. If Roxie kept it up, he could lose everything: his job and his reputation. He'd have to leave the area and start all over again. As bad as Blake had hurt me, I couldn't help but feel guilty.

That durn Janine. I needed to send her a text and tell her to stop praying. I hadn't expected her prayers to work so quickly and she was messing up my plan. I needed her to stop bothering God so He would stop bothering me. At least until Roxie got to step number ten.

I waited until everyone left and finally made my way home. I pulled a Lean Cuisine out of the freezer for Sunday dinner. It wasn't like I was trying to lose weight, but frozen dinners were the cheapest way to go and I was all about saving money these days.

I spent the rest of the afternoon watching movies on Lifetime and ignoring calls and text messages from Janine. She said she thought she would have seen me at church and wanted me to go out to eat. She also wanted to know if I had talked to God about everything that was going on and if He had answered. And she wanted me to know that she was still praying for me. I refused to answer her. The guilt from the church service was bothering me enough. I didn't need Janine to make it worse.

What was really difficult was ignoring God. I could almost feel Him tapping me on the shoulder, wanting to talk to me, but I just sat there on the couch, pretending I didn't feel Him or hear Him.

Me and God had a funny relationship. I remembered Roxie's attitude from my early years of growing up. It wasn't that she didn't believe in God. In fact, I think she believed in God so much that she thought it was best that she stay far away from Him because of all the dirt she did on a daily basis. So in the early years, we never went to church, never prayed, and the only Bible in the house was the big dusty one on the living room table.

When Roxie left, my grandmother made sure I was in the church every time the doors opened. She figured she hadn't done a good job of raising Roxie and wanted to make sure I turned out differently. After Roxie left, she made a lot of strict rules about music, television and movies, boys, everything. In her eyes, the last thing I needed was to end up being a rank heathen like my mother.

I really enjoyed going to church as a teenager, probably because I had lots of friends in my youth group and choir. There were a couple women in the church who must have felt sorry for me, and took me under their wing as a daughter, especially since Grandma was always working. So I enjoyed the fellowship of a church family.

But God? I had to admit that I always kinda kept Him at arm's distance. I couldn't understand why a God who was supposed to be so loving and so good could let bad things happen to me. How could it be that I never even met my father? That my mother honestly admitted to me and my grandmother that she didn't even know who he was? How was it that my mother, who I adored and loved to spend every waking minute with, could just leave me like she never loved me?

Me and Roxie used to have the most fun. We'd spend every Saturday in the kitchen with Grandma, cooking Sunday dinner and the best desserts you ever wanted to taste. That's how I learned to make German chocolate cake. That was my favorite, but I could bake any cake or pie better than anyone I knew, even the old mothers in the church.

When Roxie would get in from her late-night escapades, she'd climb into the bed we shared and tickle me until I woke up. She'd tell me all the stories of what she'd done. I'd be excited and horrified at the same time. I'd always swear I'd never grow up and be like her. But at the same time, she fascinated me.

Every day after school, she'd be waiting for me. We'd walk home and stop at the park. She pushed me on the swing forever, and then we'd slide down the slide and she'd ride on the merry-go-round with me, even though she was a grown woman. When we got to the house, she'd do most of my homework so I wouldn't get yelled at when Grandma came home from work.

Every once in a while, Roxie would get a job and I wouldn't see her as much. It never lasted for more than a few months though. She always found some reason to quit, or got in a fight with someone and got fired. Or got caught sleeping with someone and had to leave before she got fired.

Whenever she wasn't up under some man, it was always me and her. Having fun, laughing, and getting into all kinds of trouble that my grandmother said would kill her before her time.

Until Mr. St. James came along. Then I started seeing her less and less. When it seemed like they were getting serious, she'd try to include me on their dates, but he always acted like he didn't want me around. One night when he brought her home, I heard them arguing in the living room about how he never wanted children—not his own, and especially not any other man's.

The next day when I woke up, she was gone. I didn't see her again until my grandmother's funeral.

So even though I knew it was important to do right and serve God, I never really got over the fact that He took away the two women I really needed in my life at important times in my life. I served Him because it was the right thing to do, but I didn't take it overboard like Janine. All that praying and helping people was too much to ask. I figured as long as I didn't commit any of the big sins, me and God should be straight.

I flipped through the channels trying to drown out a nagging realization. Not only did I need to forgive Blake and Roxie. Maybe I needed to forgive God, too.

Chapter Thirteen

Blake's day off turned into almost a whole week. I guessed he couldn't bear the thought of being at work while he was wondering whether he had HIV. I knew he had to be scared out of his mind. I couldn't imagine waiting and wondering every day until those test results came back. I called him and texted him every once in a while during the week with work questions. He'd send brief answers. I probably should have been the caring fiancée and tried to press him and find out what was wrong. For real though, I was enjoying the break from being around him all the time.

While he was gone, I caught up on things at work. It was peaceful in the office, and I realized I actually liked my job. I just didn't want to be there with him. Hopefully, I could find something similar in another law office somewhere.

On Thursday afternoon, Blake called, his voice sounding completely different than it had all week. "Sabrina, dear, how are you?"

"Fine, Blake. Are you okay?"

"I am absolutely wonderful. Never better." I didn't think I had ever heard him sound so happy. *He must have gotten a call from his doctor's office and found out that his test was negative.*

"Is everything okay at the office?" he asked. "Sorry to have left you all week, but . . . it couldn't be helped. I'll be back tomorrow."

My stomach sank. I considered calling in sick the next day to avoid him.

"You have to let me make it up to you. Dinner tomorrow night at my place?"

Ugh. The last thing I felt like was spending an evening with Blake. "Of course, dear. That sounds wonderful. Should I order something to be delivered?"

"I'll have Bella cook something for us before she leaves. See you about eight?"

I crossed my eyes and let out a deep breath, but made my voice cheerful. "I'm looking forward to it."

I hung up and thought about how his voice sounded. He was almost . . . kind. I wondered if spending the week at home thinking he might have a scary disease had made him think about himself and maybe have some sort of change of heart about the way he'd treated me and his other women.

A few minutes later, Paris approached my desk with her gossip face on.

"Hey, Paris, what's up?" I really didn't want to hear what she had to say, but it was honestly the only way to get rid of her. I rearranged several briefs on my desk and opened a file on my computer. Maybe if I looked busy she'd spill the info quickly and then go away.

"Nothing. Just came by to say hi."

That was her technique when I was supposed to beg the information out of her. "Okay, then. Hi, Paris. Thanks for stopping by, but as you can see, I have tons of work to do."

"For now," she said, baiting me.

"What do you mean, 'for now'?"

"Nothing." She pressed her lips together with a too-serious look on her face.

"Paris, I'm not in the mood. If you have something to say, just say it. Otherwise I'd really like to get back to work."

She looked offended. "You're being pretty rude for a person who's about to be unemployed."

Now she really had my attention. I turned away from my computer monitor and stood, facing her. "What are you talking about?"

She smirked. "Come on. You know what's been going on around here. Wonder Boy has completely fallen apart. First that fiasco with those . . . things from that . . . store. And then the magazines. And then blowing that huge Peterson account. And now rumor has it that something happened Sunday at his church that makes his integrity questionable. And you know in this business integrity is everything."

My mouth went dry and my hands started to shake. Apparently I was finally giving Paris the reaction she came here for. "All I'm saying is, instead of planning to move to that fancy partner office, you may want to start looking for a new job. Because your man's days here are numbered."

My eyes flew open.

"Please, Sabrina. You think I don't know?" Paris rolled her eyes and walked away.

Those guilty feelings flooded me again. I looked up at the ceiling, wanting to talk to God but feeling so awful about what we had done that I couldn't think of anything to say. I had to tell Blake what was going on. If he knew what was coming, maybe there was some way he could salvage his position at the law firm.

More importantly, I needed to talk to Roxie. I never knew when the next revenge step would be executed and I needed to stop it before it started.

Chapter Fourteen

Roxie seemed all too happy when I called her and told her we needed to talk. She was busy that evening but said we could get together the next day. I decided to call in sick since Blake would be back in the office. If my days at the company were numbered, I might as well use up all my sick time.

When I arrived at Roxie's place, I stood outside her door for a few minutes, not sure what to do. I wanted to tell her to end the whole thing. Even though Blake treated me—us—so badly, I didn't want to go a step further with her ten steps to revenge. I would say thanks for all her help and say good-bye.

After she opened the door, Roxie studied my face as I stepped into the foyer of her apartment and stood there without talking.

"What?"

"Nothing." Roxie turned slowly and walked into her kitchen, indicating with a nod of her head that I was supposed to follow her. She had on a beige lounging outfit with an apron tied around her. "Come on in the kitchen."

Stepping into the kitchen with her brought back memories. Sweet memories. Her kitchen was sleek and modern with stainless steel appliances, black marble countertops, and dark, hardwood floors. There were a few things that didn't quite fit the art deco décor. There was a set of country-looking cookie jar canisters, just like the ones we used to have in Grandma's kitchen in our old house in Annapolis. The old spice rack, bread-box, and cast iron skillets looked exactly like the ones Grandma used to have.

I saw Roxie watching me take it all in. "Just a few touches can make it feel like home, huh?"

I nodded without saying anything. There was a big picture of Grandma on the wall over the eat-in kitchen table. I stared at her for a minute, feeling the pain of los-ing her all over again. Seemed like my life ended when she died. I had been lonely since the day I watched them lower her into the ground.

"Where'd you get that picture? All this stuff?"

"I took a few pictures when I left." Roxie looked around the kitchen. "Other stuff I've collected little by little over the years. Anytime I saw something that re-minded me of her . . . of you, I would pick it up."

I nodded.

"I know you think I left without looking back and without thinking about you two, but I didn't. You were always there with me. In my heart."

I didn't want to feel anything, but ever since Janine started praying, I couldn't seem to make my heart as hard or cold against Roxie. "So what's the plan for this evening?" Even though I wasn't as angry, I still didn't want to be all mushy with her.

She smiled. "We're gonna bake a cake. Just like old times." Her eyes twinkled. "You said Blake's favorite was German chocolate, right?

I frowned. "Yeah. Why?"

She smiled that diabolical smile. "Because there's nothing like the sweet taste of revenge."

Roxie went to the cabinets and started pulling down ingredients. "Here, help me with this." She pulled out a large mixing bowl identical to the one that Grandma used to bake all her cakes and pies with.

My eyes widened.

She laughed. "Brings back memories, huh?"

I nodded.

I started quietly sifting flour while Roxie creamed a few sticks of butter. I knew we were both remembering our baking Saturdays in the kitchen with Grandma. She would teach us all her best recipes and we'd spend all day in the kitchen laughing, eating, listening to Grandma's stories from when she was a little girl, and hearing Roxie's tales of the life she would live when she left Annapolis.

"I guess you ended up with the life you always wanted, huh?"

Roxie looked up and a sad smile crossed her face. I knew she was reliving the same memories when she answered me without skipping a beat. "Yeah, I did everything I ever thought I wanted to do. But looking back, I missed out on what mattered most in life."

I measured out the baking powder and added it to the flour.

Roxie measured out cocoa powder and set it aside. "I always wondered what you were doing. Where you were. How your life had ended up. I know you don't believe me, but there wasn't a day that went by that I didn't think about you."

I greased and floured the three round cake pans Roxie had pulled out. Grandma was famous for making huge three-layer cakes that melted in your mouth. I could never eat a whole piece. Blake would usually eat his entire slice and then finish off mine.

Roxie poured the batter into two of the pans and dropped them onto the counter a few times to get rid of any air bubbles. "Wanna taste?"

I smiled. "I'll lick the bowl when we're through."

"No bowl licking today. If you want a taste, you better get it now."

Roxie chuckled and I knew she was remembering how we fought over who would get to lick the bowl when we finished mixing our cakes. The smile left her face and she looked up at me. "I was so young and so not ready. That's all I can say, Sabrina."

I looked away. "Aren't you gonna pour the third pan?"

She raised her eyebrows. "Not quite yet. We need a special ingredient for the third layer." She disappeared from the kitchen and came back with a small brown bag. She reached in and pulled out a box.

I read the label and my eyes flew open. "Ex-lax? Oh my goodness, Roxie."

She laughed that deep, hoarse laugh as she saw the shock on my face. "Didn't you say he had that big presentation tomorrow morning? This cake will be ready just in time for you to take it upstairs for your date tonight. You'll eat it with him so he won't be suspicious. Just don't eat the top layer."

I laughed for a second, but then felt that twinge of guilt. I didn't say anything for a few minutes and watched Roxie melt the ex-lax and mix it with the remaining batter. She poured the mixture into the third cake pan and put all three pans in the oven.

"Now, you go into my bedroom. There's a box on the bed for you. Put that on and I'll be there in a few minutes after I clean up this mess."

I frowned at her. She smiled and shooed me away. "Just go. It's the room on the left."

I walked into Roxie's bedroom. It was a larger bedroom than I would have expected for a condo. It had a main area for the bed and nightstand and stuff and then a little sitting room off to the side. She had a large bed with a satiny red comforter covered with pillows. On the bed there was a large white box.

I opened it and pulled out a beautiful red dress. I looked at the tag and saw it was a size four. *Roxie bought me a dress?* There were also some red pumps in the box, higher than I would have ever dreamed of wearing, and some beautiful red and silver jewelry. I quickly slipped the dress on. It fit a lot closer than the clothes I usually wore and the clinginess of the material made me wonder how much of me I was showing. The fabric was rich and silky and I wondered how much Roxie had paid for it. I sat on the bed for a second, remembering how much Roxie used to love to bring me the cutest outfits, shoes, and jewelry when we were growing up together.

I looked over into the sitting room and noticed a familiar book on a small nightstand. It was Grandma's old photo album that had gone missing the day Roxie left. I walked into the room and picked it up and started turning through the pages. There were lots of pictures of me at all different ages. There were pictures of Grandma mixed in and several pictures of me and Roxie together.

As I turned farther toward the end of the book, I realized there were pictures of me later in life, after Roxie had left. I gasped when I saw a picture of me dressed for my senior prom, of me graduating from high school, copies of my diploma, of me about to go on my first date.

"See, I was there, sorta. . . ."

I whipped around to see Roxie standing behind me in the doorway. Her eyes glistened. "You look absolutely beautiful in that dress, Sabrina."

"Where . . . where did you get these pictures?"

Roxie walked over to stand next to me in her sitting room. "I took them when I left." She ran a finger over my prom and graduation pictures. "The rest your grandmother sent me. She mailed me packages every so often, all full of stuff about you."

My eyes fell on a little table in the corner. Perched on top was an old, raggedy brown doll with one missing eye and stringy hair. I let out a deep breath. "Mimi?" I went over and picked up my favorite childhood toy. It had also disappeared when Roxie left. I was done playing with dolls by that time so it didn't bother me that much.

"Sorry. I took her. I just needed something . . ." Roxie looked down at the floor. A tear trickled down her cheek. "I slept with that doll every night. No telling how many of my tears are soaked into her clothes. Mr. St. James fussed about it every night but I told him it was all I had left of my daughter and if the doll left, I left."

I swallowed hard. Part of me was angry. But what I felt the most was pity. Staring into her eyes, I realized that in her running off to chase her dreams, Roxie had lost what it took her too long to realize mattered the most.

She wiped her face. "Come on. We gotta get you ready for your date." She led me into her bathroom. It was huge with a shower and marble Jacuzzi tub and a double bowl vanity. She sat me down on an antique chair in front of her large mirror and pulled a makeup palette out of a drawer. She set it on the vanity and stood behind me, putting her hands on my shoulders.

We both stared at our reflections, looking at our own face in the other's. Another tear trickled down Roxie's face. She reached for the bun at the back of my neck and pulled out the pins that kept it in place. "You have such beautiful hair. Always did." She tousled it a little and made it look wild. She took a large brush and began pulling it through my hair without saying a word. More tears poured down her cheeks.

I didn't want to say a word. I felt years of anger, hatred, and bitterness pouring out of me into a puddle at my feet. I felt a sting on my cheek and realized I had tears flowing as well.

"Now how am I supposed to put you in some makeup with your face all wet?"

I smiled through my tears and wiped my face. "I don't like a whole lot of makeup."

"You don't need a lot. Just the basics."

After she finished my makeup and hair, Roxie stood me in front of the mirror. "Such a beautiful girl." She put her hands on my shoulders. "I would apologize a thousand times if I thought it would make a difference." She turned me to her and grabbed both my hands. "I missed so much, Sabrina. Please don't make me miss more. I . . . I want to be in your life again. Even if you can't see me as your mother, can we at least be friends?"

I stood there with my mouth open. I didn't know what to say. Could I forgive her? Could I let her be a part of my life?

My cell phone rang. We both stood there frozen for a few seconds and then she picked it up off the counter and handed it to me. "I'm sure it's him. What time are you supposed to be upstairs?"

"Eight o'clock." I looked down at the phone. It was Janine's number. I didn't answer it.

"I better get those cakes out of the oven and into the fridge for a second so they can be cool enough for me to put the icing on. Go ahead and put some powder on and meet me in the kitchen." Roxie gave my hair one last pat and walked out of the bathroom.

A few seconds later, a text message came through from Janine:

Just wanted to let you know that I was praying for you. God is
going to give you the strength to forgive. Promise me that when
you do, you'll share your mommy with me. Love you forever.

I sat there looking at myself in the mirror. I looked
more like Roxie than I did myself. And I had to admit
that I did feel beautiful. In spite of myself, I had turned
out more like her than I ever wanted to be.

I walked out into the kitchen as Roxie was taking
the cake pans out of the ovens. She set the ex-lax layer
away from the other two layers so as not to get them
mixed up.

"I can't do it anymore, Roxie."

She looked up at me. "Do what?"

"This." I looked down at the cake pans. "This . . . revenge thing. It was really fun at first because I was hurt
really bad, but now . . . it's not so fun anymore."

"Okay . . ." Roxie gave me a questioning look.

"I've been angry and hateful for so long and now . . . I
don't want to be angry and hateful anymore. I just want
to . . . forgive."

Roxie looked at me with hope in her eyes. "Forgive?"

I nodded.

She reached out to me and I walked into her arms.
We stood there hugging and crying for what felt like
forever. I didn't have any tears left. And when we finished, I didn't have any hate left either.

"I love you, Sabrina. Always have," Roxie whispered
into my hair. She pulled back from our embrace to look
at me. "And I'm so sorry I messed up. I was so young
and so . . ."

"I forgive you, Roxie. I forgive you."

We hugged again. When we pulled away, Roxie
wiped my face and looked me in the eye. "You sure

you're through? With this whole Blake thing? Five steps is enough revenge for you?"

I laughed and nodded. "Yeah, five steps is more than enough."

Roxie smiled. She picked up the ex-lax cake and turned it over into the trashcan. "Okay, it's done."

Her cell phone vibrated. She picked it up and looked at the screen. "Well, now ain't that something. We mighta thrown that cake away too fast."

I frowned.

"This joker just sent me a text saying he wants to come by for a quickie before his eight o'clock meeting tonight. Says he's on his way down in ten minutes. Ain't that something?"

I was surprised that I didn't feel even a flicker of anger in my heart. I shrugged my shoulders.

Her eyes twinkled and she picked up the phone and typed a text message.

"What did you tell him?" The look in her eyes made me ask.

"I told him to come on down. I figured if we're gonna end it, we might as well end with a bang."

Chapter Fifteen

Roxie disappeared into her bedroom and reemerged moments later in a sexy red dress of her own. "Have a seat in my bedroom. I'll call for you in a second." She winked and shooed me into her room.

I sat in the sitting room, flipping through the photo album. As I looked at the pictures of me, Roxie, and Grandma, for the first time I felt some peace about us all. It seemed like the huge rock of hate that I had carried around on my shoulders for years was gone. I felt light and free. Brand new.

A few minutes later, I heard a knock on Roxie's front door. I heard her shoes clacking through the foyer and I went and stood behind her cracked bedroom door so I could hear.

Roxie's voice was low and sexy. "Well, hey, baby. Why the long face? You okay?"

I could hardly hear Blake's voice as he mumbled something low.

"Well, come on in and tell Mama all about it. Can't nothing be that bad that a little lovin' can't fix it."

Their voices moved closer and I figured they must be sitting on the couch in the living room. I could hear Blake loud and clear. "I've had the worst few weeks of my life. I got called into a meeting today and found out I didn't make partner. From the way they sounded, I may even lose my job. I can't figure out who it was, but somebody in my company deliberately sabotaged me."

My heart beat faster as guilt and regret rose up in me. We had cost Blake his partnership.

"And this awful thing happened in church this Sunday and now I've been ostracized by all my friends and I've lost important social connections."

"I'm so sorry, baby, but you know you got me," Roxie said.

Forgive me, Lord. I didn't mean to destroy the man's life. We had waited too late to stop our plan for revenge. I would have to find some way to apologize to Blake.

"And then my assistant called in sick today. I think she knows with everything going on at the job that my days there are numbered. She's probably out interviewing somewhere else."

"You don't know that. Maybe she was really sick. You always talk about how dedicated she is."

"She *was*. Lately, she's not been performing up to speed. In fact she's gotten downright lazy and useless." Blake's voice got louder and I could just imagine the angry look on his face. "I took her on when she was a lowly secretary. I've made her what she is today and she has the nerve to leave me? I mean, I've helped her grow personally and professionally. You should have seen her before I got to her. An absolute mess—a silly little girl with no experience or people skills. She didn't even know how to dress properly. Now she's the best in the office. They'll probably fire me and fight over who gets to keep her."

"Hmmmm . . ." I heard Roxie say. I could tell she was biting her tongue. So much for me feeling sorry for him.

Blake's voice rose. "I'll see about that. I can ruin her name at the law firm and then give her horrible recommendations wherever she tries to go."

Roxie's voice was a little tight. "Now why would you do that, honey? That girl's been good to you. You might have helped her, but she helped you too. You told me she took you to a whole new level in the company."

"Yeah, but what good did it do me? I didn't make partner. The whole point was for me to make partner. Now that it didn't happen, she was just a waste of time."

Roxie didn't say anything, but I knew she was thinking about rescuing that cake out of the trashcan. I wasn't. Even though Blake was saying those hateful things, I was through. I didn't want to hate anyone ever again for the rest of my life.

"Anyway, I didn't come here to talk about her or any other stuff. I came to spend some time with you before this meeting. You act right and I might cancel the meeting. It's not that important anyway." I heard the couch shifting a little and wondered how far Roxie was going to take this.

Blake's voice sounded low and soft. "Roxanne, you know how I feel about you. You mean the world to me. You've been there for me through all of this. I know we haven't been seeing each other that long but . . . well, everything that's happened lately has made me realize how much you mean to me. Since my life has completely gone to hell, we should do something crazy. Roxanne, will you marry me?"

I gritted my teeth and clenched my fists. Before I could get good and angry, Roxie let out that laugh of hers, low and throaty, strong and sexy. She laughed for a good while before Blake finally said something. "What's so funny?"

"Now, honey, that's the craziest thing I've heard in a long time. Tell you what. Before we get married, there's something you should know about me."

"It doesn't matter. There's nothing you could tell me that would change my mind."

"Okay. In that case, I have a daughter."

"A child? You have a child? But surely she's grown and on her own, right?"

"Of course."

"Then why should that matter?"

"I'll let you decide." Roxie called out, "Sweetie, come on out here and meet your soon-to-be stepdaddy."

All the color drained from Blake's face when I walked into the living room. He jumped out of Roxie's arms and off the couch and stood. Roxie stood and put her hands on her hips. Blake looked at her and then at me and then at her and then at me. "You . . . You're . . ."

He walked around the couch to where I was and faced me. He was staring at me like he'd never seen me before and it took me a second to remember the hair, makeup, and sexy red dress I was wearing.

I put my hands on my hips like Roxie. "Hi, Blakey." I looked down at my watch. "We still on for eight o'clock?"

"Sabrina, what are you doing here? Why are you . . ." He looked me up and down and then turned to Roxie again. "Your daughter?"

Roxie nodded and smiled. "Ain't she just beautiful? Now that's who you should be asking to marry you." She smirked.

Blake moved back from me to a neutral position between the two of us. "How long have you . . ."

"How long have we known about you and your lying, cheating ways? Let me see . . ." Roxie stroked her chin like she was thinking. "Christine let us know about three weeks ago."

Blake's mouth dropped open and his eyes widened. "Christine?"

We both nodded. Roxie continued. "Yes, honey. Christine. And I have to tell you, Amber and Shaquetta weren't too happy about it either. We all took it kinda bad. But I can honestly say—we're all feeling better now."

Blake turned bright red and I could see the anger boiling up in him. "You . . . It was all of you? You all . . . did this to me?"

We both stood there, allowing everything to register in his brain.

"How could you do this to me? You've destroyed my life." Blake clenched his fists and walked toward Roxie. His breath was ragged and fast. I was almost afraid of what he would do to her.

She held up a hand. "Watch yourself now. You don't want to get cut, honey." Roxie smiled but her face was stone-cold serious. "And I *will* cut you."

Blake had the good sense to back up off her. He turned to me. "Sabrina, how could you do this? I thought you loved me."

I laughed, sounding almost like Roxie when I did. "I thought you loved me too, Blake. See how it feels when you find out the truth?"

His eyes hardened. "You destroyed me and now I'm gonna destroy you. You'll never work in this city again. By the time I'm finished with you—"

In one move, Roxie stepped up in Blake's face, in front of me. "Now you *really* better watch yourself. Everything that happened to you was my doing. Not hers. She came over here and asked me to stop. You see, Roxie always plots out ten steps to revenge. My sweet little daughter here got nervous at five." Roxie leaned up so close to Blake's face, she could have kissed him. "You do anything . . . and I mean anything to hurt my daughter and I'll start all over again from step one.

By the time I'm done with you, you'll never work any-where in this country again. And you might just find yourself in jail. Or worse."

Roxie pointed a finger and jabbed it in his chest. "You hurt my daughter again and I'll make sure you never stop hurting. Now I suggest you get yourself out of here and forget you ever knew me. When you get to work on Monday, you pick the best lawyer in that firm and you give them a glowing recommendation about Sabrina and make sure they take her on. Right before you turn in your resignation. And if anything bad ever happens to her, I don't care if it's ten years from now, I'm com-ing after you. And this time I won't be stopped until I'm done."

Blake pressed his lips tight together.

"And the next time you decide you want to run some women, I want you to remember Roxie, hear?"

Blake turned on his heels and stormed toward the foyer. After he slammed the door, Roxie burst out into laughter. I just stood there. She walked over and took my hands.

"You okay, sweetie?"

I nodded. "Yeah. As long as I stay on your good side." We both laughed. She took me in her arms and I let her hug me. I squeezed her real tight and said, "Thanks, Roxie."

"Anything, anytime." She stepped away from me and said, "Well, I guess since you don't have your dinner date, you'll be going on home?"

I smiled and took her by the hand. "I thought I might stay around. And eat my favorite cake with my mama."

A Piece of Revenge

Rhonda McKnight

Chapter One

I downshifted the gear and maneuvered my car into the left lane on I-10. I couldn't get downtown fast enough. "Four dollars and eighty-three cents." The thought of the balance in my bank account gave me a 600-horsepower burst of adrenaline that not even a Lamborghini could match. I wasn't driving a sports car, not even close, so I had to use my good old "Tamera Watson" foot pressure on the gas pedal to push my late-model, "needs service and new tires" Honda Accord just above the sixty-five mile-per-hour speed limit. Dang computer glitches. They had robbed me of my joy this morning. I wanted to see the balance the account had grown to. I wanted to celebrate the clearing of the final deposits I'd made from the corporate benefactors who were subsidizing The Micah Center, my dream.

When it opened, The Micah Center would be an inner-city community center for kids, the ones who wandered the streets after school and on weekends. Young lives waiting to be wasted in the drug-infested, crime-infested streets of south Phoenix. Lives like that of my younger brother who was serving the last few months of a ten-year stint for bank robbery in an Arizona state penitentiary. I closed my eyes for a second to the pain that ten years had bought me, but I could not close my heart to my brother's words.

"I didn't have anything else to do," Todd replied when our grandmother had asked him why. Why, after all she'd sacrificed to raise us after our mother died, why did he do something so foolish? *Nothing to do.* I shuddered and blinked back tears. My brother's life had been stolen, but I was determined that I would give some child something to do. Unfortunately, Phoenix Federal Bank was robbing me of the anticipation of that, them and their antiquated online banking system.

I'd tried to resolve the problem by logging out, refreshing the Web page, and logging back in to see if things had miraculously been fixed in the two-minute span of time it took to do all three, but they had not. The Micah Foundation still had less than five dollars in the account. I'd picked up the phone, dialed the customer service number, and proceeded to push the series of numbers I needed from my account ID to the last four of my social. All to be told the bank was experiencing extremely high contact volume and to call back later. They didn't even let me hold. But then I figured the high contact volume was probably due to the fact that their computers had gone crazy and moved everybody's money around while we were asleep. No matter, I'd be there in less than five minutes. Well, that was if Miss Daisy would move to the right. I groaned. I downshifted again and moved back into the center lane.

I wasn't ordinarily this impatient on the road, but I had taken the day off from work to be productive, not downtown. I had bills to pay, invoices that had been waiting for the corporate funds to become available. We could have taken care of the bills already, but my husband, Leon, had insisted we wait.

"Baby. Let's hold off until all the money is in the account. Don't you want to look at it? Don't you want to see the balance when it's at its highest?"

Leon reminded me that vision was visual, and I'd acquiesced. I shivered just thinking about the pre–bill paying celebration we'd had that night. A smile curved my lips, and a flutter filled my belly. "Ooh, that man," I whispered into the emptiness of the car. *Vision*. He had enough for the both of us. That was one of the things I loved about him. He always convinced me to think big—bigger than I dared to. So against my normal operating code, I agreed to hold off on paying the vendor's down payments.

"They'll wait a few weeks," Leon had said, and wait they had.

Today I wanted to call them all and inform them their checks were in the mail. But I couldn't yet, because Phoenix Federal was messing up. I rolled my eyes in irritation at the driver in front of me, moved into the far right lane, and made the quick exit off the interstate for Seventh Street. I ran right into a mini traffic jam. I hated coming downtown. *Maybe we should consider another bank,* I thought, reaching for my cell phone. I'd have to run that by Leon. I pressed the speed dial number for Leon's cell phone. He'd left so early this morning that I'd barely had time to kiss him. The call went to voice mail. I sighed, put the phone down, and waited until the traffic moved.

Finally arriving at the bank, I exited my car and made rapid steps to the entrance. I barely escaped being knocked over by a man who was rushing to get through the door. He looked irate and I wondered if he had a balance error too. I waved at one of the men I knew to be an assistant branch manager. He'd helped me to complete the refinance on my house.

"Ms. Watson, good morning." The assistant manager stuck out his hand as I approached.

"Good morning"—I stole a glance at his name badge—
"Ken, I have a problem that I'm sure you're aware of."
He raised his eyebrows like he had no idea what I was
talking about. "With the online bank system." I threw
my free hand up in a dramatic flair of frustration. "My
account balance is incorrect."

Ken shook his head, let my hand go, and ushered me
into a glass-encased cubicle a few feet away. "Let's see
what's going on."

I took a plush wing chair and observed as Ken clicked
on the keyboard of the computer in front of him. "Your
account number?"

"It's my business account. Tamera and Leon Watson for The Micah Foundation." I gave him the twelve
numbers I'd already committed to memory. Ken typed
some more, gave his long, thin nose an exaggerated
twist, and turned the huge thirty-inch monitor toward
me. I stared for a second. I saw something now that I
had not seen on my home computer, because it didn't
give very much information. The balance was still four
dollars and eighty-three cents, but there was a debit for
$180,000. My stomach lurched.

"That's what I mean. The hundred and eighty thousand dollars, where is it? It's supposed to be in the account. I was waiting for the last sixty thousand dollars
to clear last night, but the other hundred and twenty
had already been cleared and I shouldn't have a debit."

Ken coughed and did some more typing. "Well, Ms.
Watson, you withdrew the funds."

My stomach lurched again. I felt like I had sucked in
a room full of bad air. *Withdrew the funds.* That was
crazy. Ken was looking crazy. I cleared my throat and
started my count to ten to stop the spirit of cuss that
was fighting to come over me.

Ken spoke and interrupted me at five. "The transaction was this morning. A check was posted against the account and one hundred eighty thousand dollars in funds were withdrawn."

I shook my head. "That's not possible." I thought I said it. I wasn't sure. The room was shrinking and I felt lightheaded.

"It was taken in cash." Ken's voice was distorted like he was talking into one of those voice alerting devices. "I see the account was set up as an either or signature account, maybe Mr. Watson can explain." Ken was giving me one of those sympathy looks, the kind reserved for people whose heads turned into large lollipops with the word SUCKER written in red.

Leon, of course, he must have . . . "I'll call my husband." My legs were weak and my stomach had done a somersault, but I managed to stand. There had to be a reasonable explanation. I just couldn't imagine what it might be at this second. "I appreciate your time." I pretended to look for something in my purse to avoid extending my sweaty palm to Ken.

He seemed to sense my anxiety. "Please let me know if I can be of any assistance to you." He walked around the desk and reached into his jacket pocket for a business card. I took it, gave him a weak smile, and turned on shaky legs to walk away from him. I reached into my bag for my phone and dialed Leon's number. It went to voice mail again. I cursed under my breath and ended the call. *He did tell me he had a meeting. He must not be out yet.* I dialed again, this time leaving a message. "Hey, baby, it's me. I've just left the bank and I really need you to call me. I wanted to pay the bills today so . . . Just call me."

I took the steps to exit the bank with less assurance than I had taken to enter it. I climbed into my car and heaved a few deep breaths in and out before starting the ignition. "It's okay, Tamera. Leon's a leader." I knew he had made some type of decision that was for our benefit. "He just made it without me. Which, as the head of our home, he is entitled to do," I said and looked to the left. The driver in the car next to me was staring at me like I was a loon, because I was talking to myself. I pulled out of the parking space and maneuvered the short distance to the interstate. I debated going to Leon's office, but in the end decided to go home. Whatever Leon had decided was a good thing. My husband was a smart businessman. Everything was going to be fine. I tried to convince myself of that, but somehow the nagging in the pit of my gut told me that something was horribly wrong.

Chapter Two

"You what?" Erin Young flew out of her chair and came to stand in front of me.

"I told you, it was a joint account. I'm not thinking about that right now. What if something happened to him?"

"Something like what?" Erin yelled. "He told you he was going to the office, not the bank. He told you he had meetings today and the secretary said they haven't seen him. You've been calling his cell all day and getting voice mail and you're thinking something could have happened to him?"

I pushed my body deeper into the sofa cushion and looked beyond Erin, through the mini blind slats. I could see the sun setting over the desert on the horizon. I was starting to get a headache and Erin was making it worse. I took a deep breath and let it carry my weak protest. "Leon wouldn't take our money."

Erin guffawed and shook her head. "Girl, Leon didn't take *our* money. He took your money."

I rolled my eyes. I was seriously concerned about him and here this girl was talking crazy. My husband was not a thief. "Erin, just stop. I'm really worried about him. He could have been kidnapped or robbed. You know, somebody could have made him take that money out of the bank. Somebody who knew what we were planning. We did announce the center's opening plans in the paper. We did talk about the money we'd gotten from the grants. This was public information."

Erin was shaking her head.

"What?" I asked. "I know Leon, Erin. Somebody is keeping him from calling. Something bad went down."

"So if you think somebody took him then why'd you call me instead of the police?"

"Because you're my best friend. I'm scared and I thought you could help me make the call. I didn't want to go through it alone."

Erin shook her head. "Let me get this straight. You called me to help you get the courage to call the police to report your husband missing, or kidnapped, after he took one hundred and eighty thousand dollars from your joint account. Me, who you knew would say exactly what I'm saying right now: that the lowlife stole your money."

My cell phone rang. I made a desperate lunge for it and pushed one of the buttons without even looking at the caller ID. "Leon." The voice on the other end came through a computerized system that advised me to press the number one to hear about a great price on an extended auto warranty. I wanted to cry. *Where is my husband?*

"I can't believe you had all that money mixed together and in an account that either one of you had full access to," Erin ranted. "Don't they still have joint signature accounts in banks?"

Of course they did. I didn't dignify her rhetorical question with an answer. I couldn't believe it was after 8:00 P.M. and Leon hadn't called.

"You've only been married for five months, Tamera. You didn't even know him that long before you married him."

I rolled my eyes and popped to my feet. I moved to the kitchen, pulled the refrigerator open, and removed a can of ginger ale. Maybe it would help my stomach stop turning. I hadn't eaten all day, and I wasn't feeling well. My nerves were on edge. I looked back at Erin, who was now in an arms-crossed, feet-tapping frenzy.

I tried to block out her negative words, but I was having a war in my own head about the whole thing. My heart said, "You love him, you trust him," but my logical mind said, "Money's gone, he's missing." The logical side of me was winning, but my heart was putting up a good fight.

"I'm telling you, I know him." I reentered the family room and returned to my seat. "We have the same dream to open the center. Something is wrong."

"Yeah, there's something wrong all right. You've been reading way too many romance novels, girlfriend." Erin flopped down on the sofa, pulled the cordless phone from its base, and handed it to me. "It's time to call the police."

Chapter Three

The telephone call to the police was a waste of time. Leon had been gone for less than twenty-four hours, so they refused to take a missing persons report, but they were more than happy to refer me to an attorney. I didn't need a lawyer. I needed an investigation. Leon was a big man, almost six foot two, 220 pounds, but even a big man could be overpowered by a team of thugs. Besides, I knew there was no way Leon stole from me. He wasn't a thief. He was missing and probably in danger. I shuddered at the thought. I climbed into bed and lay there, unable to sleep, body in knots and heart frozen all night.

I was finally able to officially report Leon missing at noon on Saturday. The policeman who took the report all but snickered in my face when I'd told him the circumstances surrounding his disappearance.

"Okay, let me recap the details." The police officer moved the form he'd been writing in around on the desk. "You think your husband has been kidnapped or in an accident."

I nodded.

"The two of you hadn't talked about the money, hadn't agreed to move it to another bank, or stick it in a crate under the mattress."

I nodded again.

"Okay." He whistled low and hard. After making a few more notes, he asked, "Did he by any chance pack?"

"Pack? No." I shook my head. *This is ridiculous.* "I don't understand the question. If he'd packed would I be here saying he was missing? His clothes are still in the closet."

The police officer leaned back a bit. A smug expression came over his face. "Did your husband own anything that was really valuable to him? Photographs, books, a stamp collection, game ball? Anything that'd he'd never leave without?"

My mouth dropped open. Leon owned an autographed Michael Jordan Chicago Bulls championship game jersey. He kept it in a special fireproof case in the back of the closet. It was worth more than $3,000. He would never leave it behind. I met the cop's eyes. "Well, yes, he owns a jersey. It's worth a lot to him."

"You let me know if it's missing. I've got everything I need to put out the report."

"It's not missing." I was emphatic. "Once I confirm that, will you put out an All Points Bulletin?" I'd heard that on television. I wasn't even sure what it meant, but it seemed urgent.

"You check for that jersey. If it's there, I'll look for him myself." He winked.

I wanted to snatch him across the counter. Did he think this mess was funny? That my husband might be in a ditch somewhere was funny? "I don't like your attitude, Officer. I assure you I'll be putting in a complaint to your superior."

He shoved the papers for my report in a file, turned his back to me, and threw words over his shoulder. "We'll be in touch, Mrs. Watson."

But they weren't in touch. The weekend came and went. I'd called Leon's cell phone at least twenty times.

There was no more room in the voice mail. I couldn't believe that I hadn't heard from him, and I was really starting to think I was being a fool for believing something had happened to him.

I stood outside his closet door. When I returned from the police department, I didn't check for the jersey. I wasn't going to dignify the cop's ridiculous insinuation about Leon's character by actually looking for it. But now it was seventy-two hours since I'd last seen my husband. I had to know. I had to know, but I couldn't bring myself to turn the doorknob to his closet. I was too afraid. I was afraid that if I found Leon's jersey, someone had hurt my husband, and afraid that if I didn't find it, he had hurt me. But I had to look. If I was going to call the police and demand they step up their investigation, I had to be able to answer the question the police officer had posed to me. *"Did your husband own anything that was really valuable to him? Anything that'd he'd never leave without?"*

Leon worshipped that game jersey. He told me he was planning to have it framed, and he'd hang it in his office in the center. That is, after we had the security system installed. He would never leave it behind. I shook my head.

"This is crazy," I whispered to myself. "Leon did not steal our money." I turned the knob and pulled the door open. I bolstered confidence and stepped into the long walk-in closet, but something hit me in my spirit. It was a blow like a baseball bat against my chest that sucked the wind from my lungs. I had to fight to keep the bile down and work to move my feet, because I already knew, without reaching the area where the jersey was kept, that it was gone.

Chapter Four

I couldn't go to work, so I called in sick. Not only was I sick, but it was time to do what the police had suggested and talk to an attorney. I had a serious problem. Not only was the money from the sale of my grandmother's house gone, all $90,000 of it, but so was the money we'd raised at the neighborhood rally, and $80,000 I'd gotten from the corporations who'd given me grant funds. Only ten thousand of the money was actually Leon's and God only knows who he'd stolen that from.

"I'm trying to make sure I'm hearing you right." I shifted in my seat and blinked against tears that were burning my eyes. "You're telling me that there's nothing I can do?"

The attorney was looking at me the same way Ken at the bank and the police officer had looked at me, like I had a sucker for a head, or at least that's how I perceived it. "He has broken the law by stealing the corporate funds, but you'll have to find him first and prove he was the one who took and spent the money. He could just as easily say he removed the money for both of you."

I was getting more furious by the minute. "But he was the one who went to the bank."

"I know, but what happened to the money after that is your word against his. He could say you both agreed to take the money out. You'd have to show a trail that led to his having the money."

This was unbelievable. "His missing isn't a trail?"

"He's not really missing. He's only been gone a few days, Mrs. Watson."

"But he's not coming back. That jersey is proof that he's not coming back. He officially packed. It was just light." I sighed. This was beyond humiliating. This woman, the police officer, and Erin could not believe I had been naïve enough to trust a man I hardly knew with all that money. What they didn't understand was that I thought, really believed, that I had met my soul mate. I believed that Leon loved me. Obviously, I couldn't have been more stupid.

"I'm sorry I don't have better news," the attorney said. "Perhaps you can raise money some other way. They were matching grant funds, so you'd have to raise enough to equal the amount you received by the time you have to fiscally account for how you spent the money. You do have a year."

I stood on weak knees. A year. Was she kidding? I'd need more than that to come up with $80,000. I had to get the money back. "What if I found my husband and found the money? I could take it back, couldn't I?"

"Mrs. Watson, I advise you to contact the police and let them handle this."

"Why? So they can tell me the same thing you just did? It was our money." I pulled the strap of my handbag from the arm of the chair and turned toward the door. "I appreciate your time." I left the office.

I was so screwed. I had not only been robbed of my grandparents' inheritance, but now I was going to have a legal problem if I didn't have $80,000 in a year.

"Leon, how could you do this?" I asked in the quiet of my automobile. I grabbed the steering wheel and gripped it with all my might. It was finally going to happen. The thing I'd been fighting all morning, all weekend really. The tears I'd been keeping down in my soul were finally going to fall.

Chapter Five

I walked into my house, kicked off my shoes, and entered the small family room. More tears rolled down my cheeks. I'd had to cry without losing control as I'd driven home, but now that I was here there was no reason to hold back. I sobbed until I was hoarse and couldn't cry anymore. Not only was my husband gone, but so was my dream. The Micah Center had been stolen from me, stolen from the children I was trying to help.

"God, how could this happen? How could you allow him to steal the center? I thought this was your will." God didn't answer me. I was beginning to wonder if He was listening. I had been praying all weekend for Leon to be okay, to not be hurt, for our money to not have been stolen, but in the end it had been. Stolen by the man I thought God sent to me to be my husband.

I picked myself up off the floor. It was time for some serious therapy. Oh yeah, a sista needed to stretch out on the proverbial couch. I went into the kitchen, opened the freezer, and reached in for a pint of chocolate-fudge ice cream. I removed a serving spoon from the silverware drawer, grabbed some napkins, and headed back to the family room. I didn't care what anyone said; Sigmund Freud didn't have nothing on Ben and Jerry.

I turned on the television and aside from a bunch of stupid "who's the baby daddy" talk shows, decorating shows, and reruns of all the *Law & Order* franchises, there was nothing to watch. I wasn't used to being home in the middle of the day, and when I was, I would spend my time reading everything I could about running a nonprofit, or grant writing, et cetera, et cetera— all the things it took to take my dream to the next level.

I shoved a huge spoonful of ice cream in my mouth to keep the scream from coming out. I blinked against new tears and put the television guide back up. I noticed a title for a show that seemed to match how I was feeling: *Snapped*. I'd never heard of it before, but it looked interesting. The guide listed this episode as: "A woman murders her husband when she finds out he's cheating on her."

"Okay, I'm feeling that," I said.

An hour later I was done with the ice cream, eating Oreos, and watching the 12:00 P.M. episode of *Snapped:* "A woman murders her husband and his children think she was a gold digger. They fight until they bring her to justice." 1:00 P.M.: "A woman murders her husband for insurance money." 2:00 P.M., 3:00 P.M., 4:00 P.M., snap after snap after snap. It was a women-gone-wild murdering marathon.

The pizza man came and went and so did the Chinese delivery man. *Does this show ever end?* There was an entire underworld of murdering, and stealing wives and husbands out there. Apparently, I was lucky to be alive, because Leon was one of them.

I attempted to get dressed for work the next day, but I just couldn't. There was no way I was going to be able to concentrate, so I called my boss. "Hi, Tracey. I hate to call in again, but I really think I have the flu." I knew I already sounded horrible, but I coughed for good measure.

"You do sound bad. Stay home. The last thing we need is you coming in here and infecting everyone. I know you've been running yourself ragged getting ready for the opening."

"Yeah, I have, but I'll make sure to get caught up before taking time off," I promised, knowing the only days I'd need to take off were for grievance, and I was doing that now.

Tracey and I ended the call. I went in the kitchen and put some cut-and-bake cookies in the oven. They'd make a great breakfast. I was so bloated from eating sugar and salty food. I knew I was going to gain weight. I had a vision of my behind blowing up into a balloon every time I ate something, but I couldn't stop myself from eating and I didn't dare look at myself in the full-length mirror. I was depressed enough. I just put on a big T-shirt and crashed in front of the television.

Between the crazy movies on Lifetime and episodes of *Snapped,* I had lots of drama to fill my time. But then there were the commercials. Those stupid cruise line vacations with families and couples, and happy house-wife commercials that made me miss the one thing I wanted more than my precious Micah Center—a family of my own. I threw myself into the seat cushion and started bawling again. Leon and I were supposed to live happily ever after. We were supposed to have beautiful brown babies and raise them to be full of destiny and purpose. Our kids would literally turn the world upside down. We'd even tossed around strong, meaningful names for them. Didn't that mean anything to him? Had he been a phony or had he changed?

"Lies, deceit, murder, betrayal," the announcer on the television said. I stopped crying. It was time for the next episode of *Snapped.* "A woman's baby is kid-napped by her ex-husband." This was going to be a trip.

I settled in and watched with new enthusiasm, because this woman had done something that none of the other folks on *Snapped* had done. She'd hired a private detective. I sat up in my seat at the same time the oven was dinging to tell me my cookies were ready.

Why hadn't I thought of that? I went into the kitchen, pulled the tray from the oven, and placed it on top of the stove. *A private detective. They find people. Maybe one could find Leon.*

I found my telephone book. I opened it to the yellow pages listings for private investigators. Empowered to take control over this mess, I placed a few calls.

I got answering machine after answering machine. When I didn't get a machine I reached a receptionist who, I imagined, was filing her nails and chewing bubblegum. Were these guys legit? I let out a long sigh, went into my office with the phone book, and plopped down into the chair. There were lots of them and I was in for the long haul on finding one. I was also nervous about what a service might cost.

I had not turned on my computer in days, which was not like me. Big sign of depression. I needed to know how much money I had to the penny, so I booted up and signed on to my bank account and then my credit card account. I had about $200 in cash. No surprise there, but I didn't realize how much I'd paid down my credit card. I had $1,800 in available credit. I twisted my lips. "What are the chances I can find him with two thousand dollars?" I said, but then I shook off doubt. I knew Leon could be anywhere in the entire world, especially with nearly $200,000, but I had to try. I had to do something.

I picked up the phone and called the next private investigator listed in the book: Powers Investigations. The voice on the other end of the phone was not a bubblegum-chewing airhead. It was male and it definitely sounded powerful. It was strong, and sexy. He sounded black. *Are brothers PIs?* I was about to find out.

"I need a consultation for a . . . I need to have someone . . . found," I choked out the words.

"That's what I do," the voice said. "But I don't do phone meetings."

"I know. None of you do," I replied, thinking about the response I'd gotten from the other detectives. "You're local, so I'll be there in twenty minutes if you can see me."

"Sure, I'm making my way through paperwork. I'd love to push it aside. Come right in." The voice was so welcoming.

I looked down at my ice cream–stained T-shirt, and thought about the three days' worth of butt funk I needed to wash off and the matted mess on top of my head. "Make that an hour."

Chapter Six

Powers Investigations was located in a small, two-room space over a lawyer's office on a less-than-attractive street in downtown Chandler. I pushed the button for an elevator that looked like it had been installed by slaves. They were sorely in need of an upgrade. The building did not get me excited about Powers Investigations. I hoped he was in the habit of passing some of the money he saved on office space to his customers, because I'd been quoted some hefty prices on the other calls.

The elevator creaked and croaked, and I finally made it to the second floor. I was relieved when the door opened. I was even more relieved when I found Hill Harper or, rather, his taller, even more handsome brother standing there. My voice left me.

"Ms. Watson." He reached his hand out, and took mine. "Be careful. The step isn't even."

I looked down and saw that the elevator floor was not quite in line with the carpeted hallway I was exiting on to. I looked back up and time seemed to stop. He was staring. His soft, chestnut eyes had tiny flecks of green in the irises. They looked like topaz gemstones. The earlier apprehension left my body. It went back down to the first floor with the closing elevator.

"I'm Kemuel Powers. Most people call me Powers." He released my hand, which I needed him to do. A sista was feeling really vulnerable, and the last thing I needed was to think Mr. Powers had magical powers, or I'd be handing over my credit card hoping he'd rescue me. A good-looking man had already beat me out of my money this month.

"Let's step into my office."

We moved about ten feet to a set of doors, and passed through a small reception area that was meagerly furnished with a desk, chair, and a pitiful, floor-sized plant that was in need of pruning and water. We then entered a huge office. I gathered it took up the entire top floor of the building because it had a panoramic shape, with windows that provided views from two angles. It was dark. Not because there weren't opportunities for light, but because the blinds, like hooded eyes, were barely open, and the wood was that dark, knotty pine that could be found in the older buildings and houses in this part of Phoenix. Although large, the room was divided by a glass-beaded curtain that made it appear much smaller than it was. *Hanging beads? I didn't even know they still made those.*

"Please have a seat." He motioned to one of two club chairs on the side opposite from the chair he slipped into behind the desk.

I took in the massive wooden bookshelves that ran from the floor to the ceiling in almost every corner of the room. It looked more like a library than an office. Nearly every nook and cranny of the space was filled with books. There were hundreds of them. I wondered if he'd read them all.

Powers's desk was completely clean, except for two five-by-seven framed pictures that I could see held pictures of women; one with two boys and the other in a graduation cap and gown. The only other things on the desk were a telephone, laptop computer, a pen, and a legal pad. "Your family?" I asked, pointing at the picture of the woman with the children.

He picked up the frame. "Yes, my baby sister and my nephews. They live in Nashville. Moved about two years ago when her husband was relocated with his company. I miss them terribly." He put the picture down, chuckled, and reached for the other frame. "And this is my older sister. She's an attorney with lots of unsolicited, big-sisterly advice. I don't miss her as much."

"Local?" I asked, nervously twisting the strap of my handbag around my fingers.

Powers noticed my fidgeting and sat back in his seat. "Los Angeles."

I nodded and attempted to smile. When I couldn't manage one, I slid my eyes away from his and surveyed the rest of the office space, the side beyond the beaded curtain. A sofa, television, and small kitchenette were in residence. I wondered if Powers lived behind the glass veil.

"So tell me, Ms. Watson." His voice was deep and strong, but still gentle. It was time to get down to business. "What can I do to help you today?"

I couldn't avoid this part anymore. It was the reason I was here, so I took a deep breath and forced myself to meet his gaze. "My husband is missing." I cleared my throat. "And so is a hundred and eighty thousand dollars of money that belonged to our nonprofit organization."

Powers didn't blink. He merely nodded his head, picked up a pen, and began to take notes. "Tell me more."

"What exactly do you need to know?" I clutched my purse to my abdomen. I was about to embarrass myself with my ridiculous tale. I didn't want to tell any of it that I didn't have to.

"Everything," Powers said. "Tell me how you met him and move forward. Don't leave anything out." He smiled, and even though I hated to share my story, I couldn't help but relax as I recounted my first meeting with Leon.

"Miss Taylor, what a pleasure to finally put a face to the voice." Leon Watson of Temple Realty stuck out one hand for a quick shake and put the other on my shoulder. He escorted me into his office. "Please have a seat."

He was a tall, well-made piece of eye candy: white teeth, nice haircut, and good diction. I was in instant like. He offered me a beverage and then immediately went into telling me how excited he was to list my property. I was thrilled, because no one else had been that enthusiastic about the neighborhood my grand-mother's house was in.

"I'd like to sell it as is," I said. "The house is paid for. It was willed to me."

I had mentally gone to another place when I re-counted my first meeting with Leon. The clearing of Power's throat brought me back to the present. He was taking a lot of notes. It seemed he was transcribing every word I said, so I continued.

"I wanted to sell the house as is, but Leon convinced me that if I invested seven or eight thousand dollars in it, I could easily recoup that and another ten. He con-vinced me to take out a small mortgage on my house to pay for the renovations," I said. "He even helped me find inexpensive labor and personally assisted me with painting the rooms. Of course by then we were no lon-ger 'Miss Taylor' and 'Mr. Watson.' We were dating." *Hot and heavy,* I thought. It was me who cleared a throat this time. "Anyway, we connected from that first meeting, because he seemed to be so excited about my plans. He told me it had always been his desire to work with the disadvantaged youth on Phoenix's south side. The Micah Center was his dream too."

"So, he told you he had a small amount of money saved, continued to date you until the house sold, and then asked you to marry him." Powers's matter-of-fact tone pulled me from my memory.

I took a deep breath, looked down at my hands, and then back up at him. "That easy to figure out?"

Powers shook his head. "For me, but I'm a professional. This is what I do all day. Every day," he replied. "Except on Sundays." He smiled again and I wondered what he did on Sundays. I wondered if he was a Christian. I'd noticed he had a large plaque on the wall behind him with a scripture embossed on it. Scriptures didn't always mean people loved Jesus, but it was a sign that maybe I was dealing with someone with integrity. I wasn't trying to get robbed again.

"This happens all the time. It's very common." Powers's voice interrupted my thoughts. "I had a similar case just a few months ago." I knew he was trying to make me feel better about my foolishness, but it wasn't working. I should have thought through things more carefully. Leon really was too good to be true.

"If my instincts are correct, you may be the victim of a sweetheart swindle." Powers put his pen down and sat back in his chair. "Most of us aren't aware of the vast amounts of information we give to others when we're chatting with them. In the workplace, at the gym, on a plane, but especially in a new business relationship such as one where you're listing a home. If, in fact, you've been a victim of a con artist, men like your husband absorb every tidbit of information that you tell them. They observe things that other people don't notice. How we dress, our choice of hairstyles, the type of car we drive, what part of town we live in, and a host of other clues are given away without us ever uttering a word. After a con artist gets his prey to start talking, the game begins. They'll do and say whatever they believe the victim wants to see and hear to get close to their money."

"But I don't get it; con artists prey on people with money. I barely had two dimes to rub together when Leon and I met." *Kind of like now,* I wanted to add.

"You had property and a dream. A dream that was going to require you to turn that property into cash. You shared your plans with him in your first meeting, so he knew you weren't going to close on one house and immediately buy another. He knew the money would be sitting around in an account until you spent it down."

I shook my head. I couldn't believe that I was some type of mark from the moment Leon met me. "Isn't it possible that he met a woman and ran off with her? I almost think that would make me feel better than being completely set up."

"It's possible." Powers picked up his pen. "But not likely. I mean, you've only been married four and a half months, Mrs. Watson. You're a very attractive woman. You could easily hold his attention for longer than that. I can't imagine that he would be looking for a girlfriend so early in your marriage."

Very attractive. Those words were a shot of espresso. Boy did I need that hit, especially since I'd been thinking that in addition to his being an obvious thief, Leon's leaving had something to do with me, my inadequacies, the ones that crept to the forefront every time I met a man and every time one left me.

"Let me have his social security number and I'll do a background check." Powers picked up his pen again. "Hopefully, the one you have is his real one. We'll see what I find."

"So, you'll take my case?" My head bobbed like it was on springs. I didn't want to go through the humiliation of telling this story to another PI. Besides, he was a brother. I felt comfortable with him.

"I can," Powers said. "I have time and I think it'll be fairly easy to help you, especially if you have the right social, but even if you don't, we'll nail down who he is."

I nodded. "We need to talk about money." I gripped my purse tighter. "My husband has most of it. All I have is a credit card and there's not a whole lot of money on it."

"We can start with a retainer. I'll try to work quickly," he said as if it didn't matter how much money I had. "Just so you know the steps, I'll begin with a background check and put together a profile. I'll see if he's using any credit cards anywhere, using his ID for flights or trains, see if he's purchased a car. If I can't find him actively moving, I'll try to locate him based on something from his past."

I was overwhelmed. I couldn't believe I was sitting here talking about background checks and profiles. I was supposed to be at work, groaning about my accounts and my boss. Dreaming about the day I could sit in an office, side by side with my husband running our center, not sitting in a private investigator's office. My eyes began to get wet. I fought letting the tears fall. "That sounds expensive."

"It doesn't have to be," he replied. "Trust me, I'm fast."

I nodded. Instinctively, I trusted Powers, which wasn't really saying much, because I'd instinctively trusted Leon. But I was here and I had to try something. I reached into my purse for my credit card. "Let's get started."

Chapter Seven

My days were starting to run into each other. I hadn't left the house since I'd met with Powers. I had even let myself run out of ice cream. Erin would not stop harassing me. She was my best friend, but I was starting to wonder if she had a multiple personality disorder. Her messages were getting on my last nerve. "Girl, I told you he was no good," and "I'm so sorry this happened to you," and "We should pray." She was making me crazier than I was making myself.

Then there was Kym, my virtual administrative assistant for the Micah Foundation. We hadn't talked since Friday morning. She'd been calling and texting and sending e-mails nonstop. "Tamera." Kym barked my name and pulled me out of the fog. "Are you listening to me? I need to get the invitations out to the corporate donors. You have to approve the verbiage."

I should tell her, I thought. She was invested in this project too. Even though she was being paid, Kym had always gone above and beyond the dollars she invoiced me for, because she believed in what Leon and I were doing. *I should tell her.* But I couldn't. I just couldn't say it today. I washed my hands over my face and bit my lip.

"Tam, is something wrong?"

I forgot we were on a video conference call. I looked at my computer monitor and found Kym staring back at me. "I just need coffee," I said. "It's six A.M."

"And that's not new. We always meet at six A.M." Kym's irritation was rising. "Tamera, you've been acting strange for days. Not showing up for our meetings, and I haven't even seen Leon. What's going on? Is there something I need to know?"

I grimaced. "I just need a little more time. Some things are happening with the 501(c)." I felt guilty about lying to her. I was lying to everyone these days.

"What things?" Kym asked. "You don't even need that to open. It's not a priority item right now."

I didn't want Kym to see my face, so I reached down into a drawer like I was looking for something as I spoke. "I should have it resolved in a day or so. The lawyer is helping. Really it's minor." I sat back up to face her.

Kym held up a legal pad that was filled with items. "Then we need to get through this list."

I nodded and Kym proceeded to tell me the fifty things I needed to do in the next week to keep us on schedule for the opening. I pretended to be listening, said, "Okay, all right, sure and uh-hum." I nodded as appropriate. I even faked taking notes.

"I'll e-mail it all to you again." There was a little less irritation in her voice. "I really need you to at least approve the invitation, and the artwork today. Oh and the furniture. If you want chairs for people to sit in you have to pick them today. The supplier has a three-week delivery window."

"I hear you, Kym. I'll do all those things today."

"Make sure you do." Kym wagged a finger at me. "We'll reconvene this time tomorrow."

"Yes," I said. "I have to get dressed for work." She nodded and I pushed the mouse to end the call.

Maybe I could send her an e-mail. People broke up by text message these days. An e-mail wouldn't be too bad. I needed to get her off the payroll after all. I didn't have money to pay her to keep working for a center that wasn't going to happen. I sighed and turned off the computer. After I left the office, I slowly marched up the stairs to my bedroom and climbed back under the covers on my side. Leon's side continued to be undisturbed. I dared not stretch my body across the expanse of mattress. Doing so would be a reminder of the awful place I was in right now. *A reminder like that closet,* I thought, looking at the now closed door where Leon's possessions remained. The closet full of his clothes and shoes he apparently didn't need anymore now that he was living it up with my money.

My heart was so heavy I thought I'd die. I reached for my Bible on the nightstand and opened it to the marker I'd placed in Deuteronomy 32. I had been reading it before I fell asleep last night.

> *For the Lord will vindicate His people, And will have compassion on His servants, When He sees that their strength is gone, And there is none remaining, bond or free.*

The Lord will vindicate His people. I'd chosen that passage of scripture, because it was the one hanging in Powers's office. I thought it an odd choice for décor, even the office of a PI, but then I considered I'd been in a room where glass beads hung in a solid panel between spaces. Not that there was any bad Bible, but Powers's taste was probably in his mouth.

When He sees that their strength is gone. I read it again and thought about my situation. I needed God to vindicate me. I could only hope the scripture applied to sweetheart scams, because my strength was definitely gone. I closed the Bible, stared at the ceiling, and said a prayer. "Lord, please help me. I'm in so much trouble. All I wanted was to love my husband. Start a family and do some good for the community. How could things have come to this?"

God was silent. Hope did not engulf me. The answer to my problems did not fall from the sky. Even if I tried, I was hard-pressed to remove the layer of self-pity that was caked on my body from head to toe. My cell phone vibrated. I reached for it and opened the pending text message. It was from my graphic artist. I sighed and read:

> Hope to catch you before you start work. I really need you to approve the artwork for the posters and postcards or the price is going to go up for printing.

And so it began: phone calls from everyone. The caterer wanted to finalize the menu, the videographer and photographers were looking for their deposits, the event planner had details to discuss, including her fee. Everyone wanted money from me. Money I couldn't pay. The only thing that I owned was renovations on a building the city gave to me. We were going to lease the furniture. Leon's idea of course. I didn't quite agree with him on that, but now I understood. Greedy dog wanted all the cash for himself.

"God help me. What am I going to do?" I sat at my desk. Looked at all the e-mails and invoices that were waiting for me and began to pray between sobs. I had called in sick for the third day in a row and now I really was sick. I climbed the stairs again and looked at the door to Leon's closet. *I should just clean it out. I should just take all his stuff out and burn it at a dump.* But I didn't have the energy to do anything. After the barrage of responsibility that had fallen on me this morning, I just couldn't do anything about his stuff.

"How dare you leave this mess behind for me to clean up!" I yelled at the door. More tears fell. I crawled into bed and tried to fall asleep, but I could not stop thinking about men—all the men in my life who had wronged me, starting with my father. He'd walked out on our family when I was six. Every boyfriend I'd ever had cheated on me, my brother got himself in trouble and was in jail, and now my husband. I was a magnet for disaster with the opposite sex, a complete failure. I cried some more. Eventually the sobbing gave way to a heaviness that lulled me into sleep.

Chapter Eight

I heard it in my dreams. The phone rang again and it would not stop. House phone, cell phone, ring . . . ring . . . ring . . . I finally answered it. I didn't even take the time to look at the caller ID. My voice was so weak and my greeting so pitiful that my boss would have been convinced I was at death's door if it were her.

"Ms. Watson, I've been trying to reach you all afternoon. I have a report." Kemuel Powers's voice came through the earpiece and miraculously bathed me in warmth. The man had a power, really a superpower, that made me feel like he could save me from this horrible mess.

I sat up in the bed. "That was fast." I'd just met with him yesterday.

"I work fast." For a fleeting second I imagined that crooked smile I'd seen fall across his face when he'd attempted to make me laugh; about what I couldn't even remember now, but I remembered the smile. It was incredibly handsome. Just like old Hill Harper himself. "Look, I'm on my way out of the office. Wednesdays are my early day, Bible Study and all, but if you don't mind, I can stop by your house and share it with you. You're on my way home."

So he didn't live behind the beaded veil. That was good news. I nodded as if he could see me and cleared my throat. "Of course," I said. "Please, I would appreciate it."

Forty minutes and a quick shower later, I was letting Powers into my house. I showed him into the family room which I managed to clean up just before he rang the bell. The trash was now jammed with ice cream cartons and pizza boxes and potato chips bags. I was pathetic and I could tell I'd gained at least five pounds, because all my jeans were too tight.

I watched as Powers glided across the room and took a seat. I was reminded by his presence that I no longer had a man and, although I was nowhere near in the market to find a new one, the eating had to stop or I'd be as big as a house by the time I wanted to date.

"Leon Watson is at Roman's Palace," Powers said as soon as my rear hit the cushion on the sofa beside him.

"Roman's Palace?" I questioned with my tone.

"Las Vegas." Powers handed me a file folder stapled with a typed report. I glanced at it, flipped the page. There were pictures. "He's been there since he left Phoenix."

I was staring at a picture of my thieving husband at a card table. Grinning from ear to ear. Some cheap woman standing behind him. "You went to Vegas?"

"No, I have a detective buddy there who I pay a fee to follow up and get pictures. It helps cut down on expenses for my clients and travel for me."

I continued to flip through the pictures. Roman's Palace was clearly a five-star hotel. Gaudy, but posh. There were pictures of him by the pool, in a restaurant, in a jewelry store putting a necklace around the woman's neck. I looked down at the meager diamond on my finger, the one I was still wearing, still holding out hope that this was all a bad dream. I put the report on the sofa, stood and slid the ring off my finger, and shoved it in the pocket of my jeans. "So, he's definitely not kidnapped or dead." I whispered those words to myself and then turned to Powers. "I guess you were wrong about the other woman though."

"Unfortunately, I wasn't." Powers paused and I knew he was about to say something really foul. "Leon has a record. He's served time for theft by deception, theft by taking—both are fraud charges. He's a con man. A real professional. He's done this exact same thing before two years ago in Houston. Stole the proceeds of the sale of a house from his fiancée. He just upped the ante with the corporate funds."

I was still stuck on the "unfortunately, I wasn't" part. He'd conveniently avoided explaining that, and although I was disgusted about Leon, I was confused about where Powers was going. "What does that have to do with the woman in the pictures?"

Powers pursed his lips for a few seconds. "Her name is Delilah Owens. She has a rap sheet too. That's how I found him. The room is registered in one of her aliases. They've been busted together before. They went to the same high school. Graduated the same year."

My stomach flipped and my hand flew over my mouth. I was going to be sick. I was going to vomit three days worth of pizza, Chinese food, and ice cream. Tears filled my eyes; anger burned the inside of my nostrils. I felt the room spin and then Powers's powerful hands gripped my arm and back. "Have a seat." His breath whisked past my ear. Like a spell it instantly quelled the nausea. "I know this is a shock."

I sat and burst into tears. Powers joined me on the sofa again. He must have reached across the table for tissues, because he handed me a fistful. Tissues, they were everywhere in this room. I'd purchased five boxes the other day because I couldn't stop crying. I peeked out of the corner of my eye at Powers. He looked so uncomfortable. He was probably used to delivering this horrible news from across a desk in his office, but now he had a weeping woman next to him. I stood and walked across the room to the window where I could blow my nose without ruining his eardrum. I pulled myself together and stopped the waterworks, which was easy to do, because another emotion was taking over.

Leon was a professional con artist and he'd known that hooker in the pictures since high school. Steam was rising in my belly. Anger was boiling in my blood. He'd married me, lain in the bed with me every night, made love to me, learned all my fears and my secrets, so he could con me out of my grandmother's inheritance. *Oh heck no.* The crying was stopping right now. "That bastard."

"Ms. Watson, I think it's time for you to consult an attorney."

"Tamera," I said. "Please call me Tamera, and I already have." I turned back to look at him. He was standing also. "I talked to an attorney. She didn't have anything to say that I wanted to hear."

"You can press charges. I think the evidence that he's got a track record of this will prove you've been a victim."

I took a few steps, closed the space between us. "I don't want to be a victim," I said. "Do you know of any way I can get money back? And I'm not talking the way an attorney would advise me."

"Something an attorney wouldn't advise you to do?" Powers frowned, but I could tell he knew what I meant.

"I know it's wrong," I said. "I know I shouldn't be trying to take matters into my own hands, but I have to try something. My mother and grandmother raised a fighter. I'm not this woman who lies down and gets swindled. I fight back."

Powers swallowed noticeably. "Things like this sometimes get out of hand and I don't want to see you get hurt any more than you've been hurt."

I didn't respond. Our eyes met for a moment and he seemed to be assessing me. "I know I sound unstable, but I'm not. I am acting in faith. I trust God to take care of me. To vindicate me and make this right."

Powers nodded. I sensed he was thinking about the scripture in his office.

"Getting the money back is the way to make it right," I said. "So, please tell me what to do."

Powers sighed like he knew I was going to ask him this difficult question. He answered like he'd already thought about the answer. "I'd have to know where he was keeping it first, and then there's the matter of getting him to hand it over. He's not likely to do that willingly."

I shook my head. "I'm not concerned about him being willing. You find the money. Can you do that? I have about a thousand dollars left and I get paid next Wednesday. That's another thirteen hundred if I don't eat." I attempted a smile. "If you find the money I'll take care of the rest."

Powers looked mystified. "How are you going to do that?"

"I'm still his wife. The same way he was able to take all as my husband, I can take all as his widow."

"Widow?" Powers's eyebrows knit together.

"Yes, widow, because after I get my hands on my money, I'm going to kill that lowlife thief."

Chapter Nine

After Powers delivered the bad news about Leon, I'd watched a few more episodes of *Snapped* and realized if I was going to kill Leon, I had to have a gun. I shifted on the sofa, and like the princess and the pea, I felt my wedding ring in my pocket under me. Leon had paid $1,200 for the rings, so I knew I should be able to pawn them for at least half. Boy, was I in for a rude awakening.

"I'll give you four-fifty," said Big Al of Big Al's Pawn and Loan. He scratched his belly as he examined my diamond through an eye lens.

"Four-fifty," I protested.

"Lady, this is barely a carat. I got rings coming out of my ears in here. Four-fifty is it."

I looked over Al's shoulder at the gun case. "I want one of those." I nodded. "Since you're not willing to negotiate with me can you throw that in the deal?"

Al laughed as he pulled a set of keys from his pants pocket and opened the case. "Live in a bad neighborhood?"

I smirked behind his back. He removed a gun from the very back of the cabinet. "Smith & Wesson double action .45," he said. "Lightweight. Perfect gun for a lady and that price is a steal."

The gun's obscure location in the case was an indication that it probably was stolen. He put it in my hand. It didn't feel that light. It felt like trouble. "Does it work for sure?"

"I don't sell stuff that don't work. You need to take some lessons on how to use it so you don't kill yourself. Shooter's Galaxy has classes."

"What about bullets?" I asked, putting it on the counter.

"You have to get your own ammo. You can get 'em anywhere." He reached back in the cabinet and pulled out a silver case about the size of a netbook computer. He opened it, removed a small cylinder, and dropped it in my hand.

"What's this?"

"A silencer. Muffles the sound of the bullet. Came with the gun. Both these and the case are yours for the low asking price of four-fifty."

I hesitated before asking my next question, because this was where it was going to get sticky. "Can I have it today?"

Big Al shook his head. "You gotta fill out a form and I need to do a NICS check."

I put a hand on my hip. "NICS check. Come on, seriously, Al, do I look like a criminal? I mean, really take a good look."

Al eyed me suspiciously and then said, "I'd have to say yes, because you look like somebody trying to break the firearm laws. That's a crime."

I pursed my lips. I'd done some reading online and it was common knowledge that the pawnshops in Phoenix were negligent on background checks. In fact, they didn't even log in some of their gun purchases just in case they wanted to sell them off the books, hence mine coming from the back of the cabinet. One could learn a lot reading messages boards on Internet forums. I wasn't going to be the only one in the state buying a gun on the straight and narrow, not when I didn't have time for the formalities. "I need it today," I said. There was resolute finality in my tone. The type of finality that said we were doing business my way or not at all. I let my eyes do a sweep of the empty store. Al's eye's followed mine. "It looks like you could use the business."

Al's bushy miniature squirrel's tails for eyebrows came together. Suspicion laced his tone. "What's so urgent?"

"I live in a bad neighborhood remember?" I said tersely. "Look, I can try to find another shop."

Big Al shook his head as if saying "no need," and then he slid my weapon across the counter. "You kill somebody and I don't know you."

I smiled, put the gun and the case in my oversized shoulder bag, and left the shop. Al didn't have to worry about this gun. It was headed for Las Vegas, and if I killed somebody there, I wouldn't even know myself.

Chapter Ten

Bang! Bang! Bang!

"Pull your shoulders back and straighten out this elbow." Bruce, my shooting instructor, helped position my arms. I squinted to improve my view of the black-and-white bull's-eye target down the range and fired off another round. I was getting used to having this hard, black metal in my hands. At first it felt like a bug, like something that crawled up my arm that I needed to shake off. But now, almost four hours into my second session of the "Basic Shooting" lesson, it was feeling like an extension of my hand.

"You sure this is your first gun? You're pretty good." Bruce winked at me.

I smiled and shifted my feet to adjust my weight. "My first time," I replied. "I think I like it."

"Most women do. It's the power. You chicks dig it." Bruce laughed and I tried not to be insulted that a kid in his early twenties had just called me a chick.

"After this, you've got one more round." He moved on to another student. I was glad to see him go. I didn't need him anymore. I had this hitting-the-mark stuff down to a tee. I had gotten used to the recoil when I fired. I had gotten used to the noise. I had gotten used to the idea of firing a gun, period. I inserted a new clip of blank bullets and pushed the start button. My target flipped down and up popped the last round Bruce had told me about. The one with figures of men and women moving; targets that challenged me to shift and move and shoot. I imagined Leon and his skank girlfriend, Delilah, and pulled back on the trigger.

Bang! Bang! Bang!

I blocked out the voice in my head that said, "Vengeance is mine," because I had a piece of revenge right in my hand. One that was sure to get me results here and now, not in five or ten years or in the afterlife. My targets were on the move again.

Bang! Bang! Bang!

My bullet clip was empty. I removed my protective eye and ear gear. The paper bodies down the lane were full of holes in all the right places. I smiled. Both of those no-good Negroes were dead.

I pulled into my driveway and noted a car rolling in right behind me. Erin. I'd been lucky she'd had to go to Denver last week for a training conference, but now she was back and I was about to get an earful. I cracked my car door and grabbed my bags.

"Are you out of your mind?" Erin yanked my poor Honda's door back like she was trying to pull it off the hinges. "Do you know how many times I've called you?"

How could I not know? She'd called me almost as many times as I'd called Leon when he first went missing. I stayed calm, hoping it would diffuse her temper. "I left you a message."

She stepped back to give me room to climb out. "Girl, you don't leave me no message on my voice mail. I've been worried sick about you and the whole Leon the Loser situation. I can't believe you didn't take my calls."

I pushed the key fob to lock my car and turned to walk to the house. She was right behind me. "Erin, I know you like to be kept up to date, but really, I've been pretty busy cleaning up the mess Leon the Loser, as you so eloquently put it, left behind."

Erin grabbed my arm and stopped me in my tracks. "It's not about being kept up to date. You're my best friend. I'm worried about you." She released my arm. "How could you be so insensitive, Tam?"

"I know, I'm sorry." I avoided meeting her eyes.

"And I'm told you haven't been to the office all week."

"I went to the doctor on Friday. I have a note. I'm out with the flu." We entered the house. I dropped my bag on the kitchen table and pulled the oversized T-shirt I'd been wearing over my head. Erin was still on my heels like a little poodle that wasn't getting its owner's attention.

"You need to get your butt back to work. I know you were planning to quit eventually, but *surely* now you need it." "Surely" had lots of emphasis on it. Erin's eyes swept my body. "And where are you coming from looking like one of Charlie's Angels?"

I looked down at my all-black spandex outfit and sneakers. I did look like a ninja, but I sure wasn't going to tell her I'd been at Shooter's Galaxy. She'd really think I'd lost it. "I was working out." That much was true. My arms were killing me. "The doctor's note will have me covered. I have more than enough sick time."

Erin's fist went to her hips. "Working out. Since when do you work out?"

"Since I have about five hundred percent more stress." I opened the refrigerator and pulled out a bottle of water. "Would you like one?"

Erin looked at her watch. "No, girl. I have to go. I've got to get my hair tightened and then I have a voice lesson." She reached up and scratched her head. The entire monstrosity of a weave moved with her fingers.

I walked closer to Erin and hugged her. "I'm sorry. I should have talked to you. I've just been in a funk. I needed some time to get my head together. I'm feeling much better."

"Yeah, you're looking pretty good for somebody's that's been beat out of one-eighty." She pulled her purse higher on her shoulder. "Did you talk to a lawyer?"

"I did. Not much I can do." I turned her in the direction of the door. "I'll tell you all about it later. Go get your wig done; nothing worse than a loose weave in the choir stand."

Erin pulled the front door open and stepped through. "I'm going to ring you after my lesson. Don't ignore my call, heifer."

"I won't."

"And don't forget I'm singing a solo tomorrow, so I expect you to be in church."

"I will."

"And wear something a little clingy." She sized up my attire again. "Who knew you looked like J. Lo under those old ladies suits."

I smirked. Erin walked out and I let my body fall against the door. *Church. No way.* I was not doing well with people. I felt like everyone could look at me and tell what a fool I was. I had a scarlet letter made out of a big fat "F" on my forehead. People would be asking me about the opening and I just . . . couldn't. I couldn't tell them the entire thing was off. The whispering would begin and the rumors would start flying. I wasn't going back to church yet. Not until I got the money and re-strategized. I needed to hear from Powers.

I walked into the kitchen and lifted my handbag off of the gun case. I opened it and took out the sleek weapon. I'd done good today. *Maybe I should have been a cop.* Guns were fun.

Vengeance is mine. There was that voice in my head again, making me second-guess myself, and filling my soul with guilt.

"I don't want vengeance, Lord. I just want my money." I knew God wasn't exactly trying to hear that crap from me, but I had to get the money back and I didn't expect some angel to drop out of the sky and hand it to me, not after the way I'd so foolishly let my husband have it.

Before God could say something else, the doorbell rang. *Erin. What did she forget?* I put the gun back in the case and looked around. Erin hadn't had anything but her purse and it was on her shoulder when she walked out, so that meant she had something else to say. I pulled the door open. My breath caught in my throat. It wasn't Erin.

Chapter Eleven

"Not a great way to open your door." I moved aside and Kemuel Powers stepped in. "Lot of home invasions in Phoenix and most happen in the daytime."

I shook my head. "My best friend just pulled out and I assumed it was her coming back."

"And that's something people scouting for a home to break into look for—recent visitors leaving. They know you'll think the doorbell is the person returning."

Sufficiently chastised, I nodded. I gushed inside though. Something about a man lecturing me was sexy. Reminded me of Leon, minus the new bull's-eye I'd permanently etched on his forehead.

"Sorry, I slipped into cop mode." He flashed me that crooked smile I'd come to love seeing. "Ten years on Phoenix PD."

"I should have guessed you'd been a cop. Isn't that where most PI's come from, the police force?"

"Yeah, I'd say about seventy percent of us do."

A moment passed between us when neither of us said anything. I noticed his eyes traveled the length of my spandex-clad body. I was wishing I still had on my T-shirt, because suddenly I was feeling exposed. He could see every curve of my "twenty pounds over-weight" body. I broke the silence. "Did you have an update for me?"

Powers was startled out of his daze. He reached into his jacket pocket. "I'm sorry. Of course. That's why I'm here. I forgot to charge my cell phone, so I thought I'd just take a chance—"

"It's okay." I nodded. "I appreciate the personal service." He was staring again. "Let me just go change."

"No." The word came out of his mouth like a rocket. I raised an eyebrow. "You're fine." His eyes fell to my hips. "Really fine—and I won't be long at all."

I swayed an open hand in the direction of the family room. "Let's sit."

He looked past me, into the kitchen. "Actually, if you don't mind, someplace where there's a table."

I remembered how uncomfortable he seemed on the sofa next to me. His long legs didn't have any place to go and then there was the crying. I could see how the space might have seemed intimate. He probably thought I was going to freak out again.

"The kitchen." I turned, and he followed. I was self-conscious about the fact that my spandex-wearing Beyoncé-wanna-be bootie was bouncing in front of him. I was glad it was a short walk. We entered my kitchen and as we did I saw the gun case. Powers would know exactly what it was, and being a crackerjack detective, he wouldn't miss it. I tried to put my body in between it and him. As he was taking a seat I shoved it back under my handbag. *Too late.* I could tell by the frown on his face that he'd seen it. "It's a precaution," I said, answering the question that lingered in the air.

Powers reached for his tie knot and loosened it slightly. I wondered where he was coming from in a shirt and tie. "I know I may sound like the poster boy for an anti-NRA campaign, but guns are dangerous."

"I took lessons." I crossed my arms in front of me.

Powers frowned. "That doesn't make them any less dangerous."

"I'm a good shot for a newbie. Even my instructor said so." I pulled the refrigerator open and removed two bottles of water. I placed one in front of Powers and slipped into the chair across from him. Powers stared me down, and I added, "Being conned has left me feeling, I don't know, vulnerable. Having the gun has helped me regain confidence."

He shook his head. "A gun is not the place to find confidence."

I took a long sip of my water. I was stalling. The confidence thing had been a lie and I sensed he knew it, so I decided to be honest, to unearth my shame. "I have to fix this situation. I need to confront Leon, if for nothing else than to look him in the face after what he did. He made a fool of me."

"You're not a fool." Powers was quick with his words. It felt like he meant them. Our eyes connected and then he looked away before he returned his gaze to mine. "You're being too hard on yourself. I'm telling you I do this for a living. I know a silly woman when I meet one."

"I handed over my life savings and money that wasn't even mine. Please, if you don't see a fool, then tell me what you see when you meet someone who allows themselves to be shanked out of their money?"

He washed his face with his hand. He seemed to be considering his words. "When I look at you, I see someone who's strong. You haven't fallen in a bottle or tried drugs. You're not lying in bed, sleeping it away or worse. You're standing, thinking, and planning. Heck, you hired me." He smiled. "I'm impressed."

"But—"

"No buts." He threw up a hand in protest. "Please, stop beating yourself up and let me tell you what I know." He reached into his jacket and pulled out a typewritten report. "I just got back from Vegas," he began. "As I explained before, I broker services from other PI buddies for the preliminary work—you know, locating the person, taking pictures and such—but then I do my own surveillance."

I nodded understanding and Powers continued.

"I followed your husband for three days. I hate to tell you this, but he's spending money like a fool. Gambling, eating high, letting the woman shop. He'll be broke inside of a few months if we don't get it back."

I noticed Powers said "we," which felt good. I'd been feeling so alone in this, but it still didn't take the sting out of Leon letting the woman shop when he'd been so cheap with me. *We're saving for our future.* How many times had he told me that?

Powers continued. "I followed him to a bank. He doesn't have an account, just a bank deposit box. I have a source trying to find out if it's in his name."

"How do you know he doesn't have an account?" I asked.

"I'm having a source check, but my guess is no account. He's stupid, but not that stupid. You could find a bank account. Boxes aren't as easy to find. Plus when he went in the bank, the clerk escorted him straight to boxes."

I nodded. This was progress. At least we knew where the money was. "What if it's in her name?"

Powers raised an eyebrow and I got question and statement in the furrow.

"Yeah, I know. He's stupid, but not that stupid."

"Probably not," Powers added.

"Well." I stood and put my hands on my hips. "I guess I'm going to Vegas."

"That's not necessary. I'll be going back. I hope to hear about the bank account on Monday. I'm trying to find out if it's in one of his aliases."

I shook my head. "I can't afford to pay you anymore."

"Don't worry about the money. Let's call your attorney on Monday. We can have her file an order to seize the box."

"The box that we don't know whose name it's in? And as for the bank account, Leon could have another identity by now. Don't you think it's likely he would with all the alias names you had in the background report?"

Powers's skepticism was all over his face. "It's likely, but, Mrs. Watson, you can't just show up and expect there not to be an altercation."

I lifted a brow. "I'm not Mrs. Watson. I never was." It hurt to say the words. "I was someone he met and took advantage of."

Powers shook his head. "I'm just trying to remember what I'm doing here." Once again our eyes locked. He cleared his throat. "I mean, I'm trying to stick to a strategic plan. That's what PI's do. We plan."

I nodded understanding, but I heard what he said. Trying to remember what he was doing here. My heart was thudding.

"Mrs. Wa—"

"Please, call me Tamera." My voice was husky.

"Tamera, I can't in good conscience let you go deal with this by yourself. Plus, I mean, you used the word 'widow' last week and now you have a gun."

If I hadn't noticed he was looking past me at my bags on the counter, I would have lingered on the fact that he'd actually said my name. It was the first time and coming off his tongue it sounded like it was spun in silk.

I shook my head. "Forget I said 'widow,' because if something should happen to the scum, something like a bullet in his head, then I would have said I was going to kill him and you'll be a witness."

Powers stood and took the few steps necessary to the counter. He pulled the gun case from under the bag and opened it.

"I got it from a pawnshop. I actually inherited a rifle from my grandfather, or grandmother. It was hers after my grandfather died, but it's too big to lug around."

Powers nodded. "Do you think your grandparents would want to see you in prison?" I looked down at my sneakers. Thought about my brother. "I've watched people, a lot of them women, go to prison every day over a man and some money, or a man and some woman. It happens, Tamera. Don't do this."

Tears were threatening to break. Powers's hands were on my forearms. "If you have to go to Vegas, let me go with you."

I wanted to fall into this man's arms. I was under his superpower for real. I was broke, scared, angry as all get-out, and at this moment very vulnerable to his touch. Leon and I had made love every day. I missed it. Now I knew how and why women slept with their lawyers and therapists. The need for affection was dancing on every nerve ending in my body. *Lord help me,* I thought. I moved out of his grasp.

"I have to preach tomorrow evening's service. But I promise we can leave first thing Monday morning."

Preach? "Did you say 'preach'? You're a preacher?"

"Evangelist. I'm still in ministry school. I deliver the evening message on the last Sunday of the month."

"A preaching private detective?"

"Yep." He put his hands in his pants pockets and rocked back on his heels.

"How do you do this work and then minister the Word?"

"I think this work really helps with the ministry. I mean other than a street ministry, where do you see and get closer to the problems, fragility, and fears that we have?"

I thought about all that Powers had witnessed in my life and realized he was right. He'd seen me at the lowest moment in my life. There wasn't much worse than betrayal.

"Will you wait for me?" He almost sounded like he was begging. Those lush brown eyes looked like they were.

I nodded yes. My angel had dropped from the sky.

Chapter Twelve

I reconsidered. I didn't want to involve Powers in this mess. Especially now that I knew he was Minister Powers. Not that I really planned to kill Leon or that garden tool he was held up with, but I wasn't above shooting a brother in the toe to get my money back. I'd seen Leon's toes. The man was fine, but those toes were not. That raggedy pinky toe definitely wasn't worth that much, so if a sista had to fire off a round . . . well, so be it.

I thought about calling my thug cousin Dre and asking him to come with me, but with Dre came drama. Four times in the county lockup and one three-year stint upstate, Dre was a career criminal with a hot temper. I'd end up in a shootout with the Las Vegas Police Department, the SWAT team, and Homeland Security messin' with my crazy cousin. At a minimum we'd go to prison, but more than likely, we'd be killed.

Powers wanted me to do things the legal way. Wait on the bank, get a lawyer, when I knew the only way to deal with my lowlife husband was face to face with the barrel of the .45 pointing at his chest. That was the way to get the money out of the box.

The phone rang and it was Erin. Her voice lesson was over. "Fill me in, girl," she said and I told her everything, except the part about Shooter's Galaxy.

"Dang, Tam. I was just kidding when I said he was a crook. I mean, he's a crook for real. You could have been hurt or killed. People like that will stop at nothing to get what they want."

Finally, some sympathy from my unsympathetic friend. "It's pretty deep."

"So what's up next? I mean, what you gonna do? Try to press charges or something?"

"Powers is checking on some things. We'll figure out a plan after that."

"Powers; that's a nice name for a detective."

"It's Kemuel Powers."

"Sounds like a brother. I keep hearing the word 'we.' Is he single?"

I thought about Powers and wanted to tell her how absolutely yummy he was. How tall and handsome and smart he was, his nice full lips and . . .

"Tam, is he single or what?"

She'd messed up my fantasy. "Girl, I don't know. I think so. He doesn't wear a ring, but then again, half the time neither did Leon."

"Well, you find out for a sista. I might need to hire him to check a background or two out for me."

"What's that got to do with him being single?"

"Honey, you know those cop and detective types like a damsel in distress. All I gotta do is turn on the tears and if a background check come back bad, I can slide Powers in as a pinch hitter." Erin laughed at her own joke. She was getting on my last nerve.

"I'ma go. *Snapped* is about to start and I don't like to miss the beginning."

"You need to stop watching all that craziness and get out of that house," Erin replied. "Come go to the singles service with me tonight."

Singles service. Was she out of her mind? "Good night, Erin." I hung up the phone.

It really was time for *Snapped*. The episode was about a murdering con artist. Great, the one thing I didn't want to see, but I watched it and turned off the television when it was done with a new knowledge. Con artists never stay anywhere for long. I had already decided that I was going to Vegas alone, but this new information confirmed I didn't have time to wait for Powers. Leon and Delilah had been in Vegas for over a week. They most assuredly would be leaving soon.

I picked up the phone and called Roman's Palace, and asked for Desiree Holmes, the alias Delilah was using. "Please hold for Ms. Holmes," the attendant said. I hung up before it connected because I'd found out what I wanted to know. They were still there.

I jumped up and ran up the stairs. I had to get to Vegas before they picked up and moved, before they decided to go to the Caribbean or Europe. I threw some clothes and toiletries in a suitcase and pulled the small bag down the stairs. I put an empty duffel bag inside the suitcase, just in case I needed a bag for the money. I reached for the gun case and just as I was about to put it in the suitcase, I realized I didn't have any bullets. I didn't even know where people got bullets from. I went into my office and opened my ever-trusty phone book for ammunition sales. Phoenix was a gun toter's dreamland. They sold bullets everywhere, even in Walmart, so Walmart it was. I had less than a hundred dollars in cash until I got paid again. Powers hadn't billed me for anything beyond the initial retainer, so I could still access the available funds on my credit card.

Getting bullets at Walmart was like buying anything else. I could have told the clerk I wanted soap or a DVD player and he would have pushed the box across the counter the exact same way. I got back to the house and noticed the sun was going down. I hated driving at night, plus there was the added safety risk. I was already tired. I took a long, hot soak in my tub, climbed into bed, and set the alarm for 5:30 A.M.

I was yawning and I wasn't even in the car yet. I hadn't been able to sleep last night. My nerves were on edge. I couldn't believe what my life had come to. Two weeks ago I was happily married and about to embark on the business venture of my dreams. Now I was alone, planning to shoot my husband in the pinky toe with a gun I'd purchased from Big Al's Pawn and Loan. Not to mention—broke. Flat broke. It didn't get much worse than this. Outside of an awful disease or a natural disaster, life did not shift like this in less than two weeks.

I poured coffee into my travel mug, grabbed the bagel and cream cheese sandwich I'd made, set the security system, and piled into my car. I yawned again. *Lord, how I wish I could fly.* I started the car. No point in dwelling on what I couldn't do. There was the matter of the gun and the fact that I couldn't afford a plane ticket.

I arrived in Vegas five hours later. The drive had been exhausting. I was so high on NoDoz and bad gas station coffee that I was probably going to turn into a gaudy Vegas neon light as soon as the sun went down. I pulled into the parking lot of the hotel I'd reserved for the one night I anticipated needing one. It was an inexpensive spot that resembled the French Quarter so much that it saddened me. Leon and I had spent our honeymoon in New Orleans. I'd known the hotel was named Orleans but I hadn't really made the connection until I pulled into the parking lot. I wanted to cry, but I woman-ed up.

It was just after noon and I realized leaving Phoenix so early had been a bad idea. I was exhausted, but couldn't check in to my room until three o'clock. I didn't have the energy to confront anyone right now. I'd drop from sheer exhaustion. I decided to risk that they would let me check in early, and thankfully the front desk clerk believed my glazed eyes were due to sleep deprivation and not a drug-induced high. I was sure the ten dollar tip I slid her didn't hurt either.

After checking in and entering my room, I sank into the mattress. It was unbelievably comfortable. It felt good to be in a bed that wasn't my own, because mine reminded me of my husband.

I had calls to make before I fell asleep. The first was to Roman's Palace. I asked for Desiree's room again. I didn't get an answer but I was satisfied that it was past checkout time and the lovebirds hadn't checked out. Then I sent a text to Erin's cell phone, advising her I was out of town for a couple days and would not be in church to hear her sing the big solo. I also told her not to worry. She'd be angry about both.

The last call was the office number for Powers. I told him I was in Vegas already, taking care of the business I needed to handle. I'd update him when I returned. I didn't want the man changing his schedule to accommodate a trip to Vegas that he didn't need to make. Then I curled up in the bed and fell into a deep sleep.

Chapter Thirteen

The Roman's Palace Hotel dripped with imagery and architecture steeped in the theme of Ancient Rome. Life-sized statues of naked men, women, and cherubs with bright gold headdresses were either mounted on columns or suspended from the beautiful summer sky that was painted on the ceiling. I couldn't say that it would have been my choice of hotels to stay in, but this was clearly baller-land.

It was 6:00 P.M. and I didn't want to waste any time figuring the joint out so I paid a hotel maid to tell me which floor the Royal Suite was on, and then threw more money at an elevator attendant to swipe a card that gave me access to the floor. I was greasing palms left and right. Who said you couldn't get an education watching television? I learned about tipping the help from Lifetime and *Snapped*.

I stood in the corridor outside of the Royal Suite and realized that there was no way for me to know whether or not Leon was actually inside. The place was sound-proof. I swore I could hear my own heart beating. The quiet made me nervous, and even though it was freezing all over the hotel, I was starting to perspire. The overpriced hotdog I'd eaten was doing flips in my stomach and that wasn't making it any better.

Why are you here? The voice in my head was back. I tried to push it out, but I knew this was not who I was. I was not some crazy person who had "snapped" and stood outside of suites in Las Vegas with a gun in my purse. I was a decent woman, a Christian who went to church every Sunday, was raised by women who taught me to pray and trust God. I was better than this. Tears began to burn my eyes.

Vengeance is mine, the voice said. *For the Lord will vindicate His people.* The scripture in Powers's office was another reminder that God would repay. I'd made a mistake. My stomach churned again and knew I would actually be physically ill soon. I had to get out of here. I had to go back to Phoenix. I had to let Powers and an attorney make this right.

When the elevator made it to the lobby, I rushed through the door and found the closest ladies' room and threw up. I threw up the hot dog, my pain, my frustration, my pride, and my anger. When I was done, I sat in that stall for a long time. I thought about my choices. The choice to date Leon, marry him, start the business, commingle our funds. All of these were my choices and they had been bad ones, because as much as Erin got on my last nerve with her "I told you so's" she was right; I didn't really know him for more than a few months before I was running my behind down the aisle talking about "I do." I stood to weak feet and left the restroom. I was going home.

I returned to the lobby and was just about to ask one of the staff how to get back to the parking area when I saw them. Leon and a tall, bad weave-wearing, skinny, cheap-looking heifer in a shiny red micro mini dress were heading in the direction of the main casino. Leon didn't even look like the conservative man I had been married to for the last four months. He was wearing a red sequined smoking jacket. It looked like he'd put an S-curl or some other craziness in his hair. He had an earring in his right ear, which held a huge diamond stud. He looked like a pimp and Delilah looked like a hooker. They turned a corner. I followed. I started thinking, *there have to be 300 people milling in the lobby area of this hotel, and I spotted them.* This was fate. An angel had fallen from the sky. I was supposed to get my money back.

Leon and Delilah entered an area called Restaurant Row. There were people waiting in long lines in front of all the many different eateries in this area of the hotel. They walked hand in hand until they made it to what looked like the very last and notably the most exclusive restaurant of them all. At least forty couples were in line waiting, but apparently the gold VIP card Leon waved got them to the front of the line. *No doubt some perk for being in one of those ridiculously expensive suites.* Once they were inside, I squeezed in beyond the crowd to the front and watched them through the gold-tinted window. I glanced down at a glass case that held the menu. I thought I would faint. They were easily going to spend at least $250 on dinner. If he'd been in Vegas since he left that was almost ten days in a $700-a-night suite, $200 meals, gambling, and that heifer's shopping. He was probably almost into twenty-five grand by now and no telling what they were driving. I was sick, really sick. No, I was not sick. I was angry. I was going to do more than shoot off a pinky toe. I was going to kill this bozo.

I continued to follow Leon and his woman that evening. They went from dinner to the casino, and then I lost them when the valet handed Leon the keys to a fancy sports car. No doubt they were out for an evening of spending more and more of the money. I was so angry it took everything in me to keep from pulling out the gun.

Chapter Fourteen

It was almost midnight when I returned to my hotel room, and to my surprise, before I could peel off my clothes, the phone rang. No one knew I was here. I was hoping it wasn't hotel services telling me my credit card was no good. It wasn't. It was Powers.

"When you travel out of town to kill your husband you never use a credit card. It's a trail that proves opportunity and premeditation." Powers's strong voice came through the earpiece.

I closed my eyes to the timbre of his voice. Why hadn't I married a man like this? A man who didn't steal, a man with integrity? "They told me I had to use a credit card." I sat down on the bed.

"If you'd told them you didn't have one, they would have taken cash. It's Vegas, Tamera."

"Then you wouldn't have been able to find me."

He chuckled. "I'm a detective. Credit card or no credit card, when I really want to, I can find anyone."

I melted. I was in love. This man felt like my best friend. Really, I was; or maybe I was so in hate with Leon, anyone was starting to sound good. I didn't want to talk about me. I didn't want to talk about Leon. I didn't want to talk about the money. I wanted to learn something about Kemuel Powers. Right this moment. I had his full attention, even if I was paying for it. I surmised that he was worth every dime.

"Tell me, my preaching detective, how was your sermon?"

"Great. I spoke to the youth about keeping their noses clean. About their destiny and their purpose. About not letting the devil and bad choices steal their futures."

I closed my eyes. I could hear the excitement in his voice. That message was all over me like a wet towel, but more than myself, it made me think of my brother. Todd needed to hear that sermon. He needed to hear it ten years ago. Powers was a power to be reckoned with. He was a superpower that God would use for good.

"Leon and I talked about raising kingdom kids. We were going to teach them all about destiny and purpose. In fact, our daughter's name was going to be Destiny. We were going to name our son Joshua because he would be a warrior, a real soldier for Christ." The memory saddened me so much, much more than seeing Leon and Delilah ever could.

"You'll do those same things. If that's what you want for your children, then God will bless you to have kingdom kids," Powers said. "You just have to find a real 'king' to do it with."

"I don't know if there's anyone out there for me."

"Tamera, you are an intelligent, beautiful woman and your heart is so pure. Believe me, there's a man who's going to recognize that as the treasure it is. You just have to move past this stage in your life."

"If I'm so intelligent then how did I find Leon?"

"You didn't find him. He found you," Kemuel said. "He's a professional. He preys on good people."

God, those words sounded so reassuring, so right. It felt like the Holy Spirit was speaking, trying to heal me. If he were here, I would have kissed him. "Thanks, Kemuel." I'd never called him by his first name, but what he'd said was so personal that I felt like it was okay to do it.

I heard him let out a long sigh. "Why did you leave without me?"

I wanted to answer him, "Because of any number of reasons: I'm stupid, I don't think right, I'm a big fat loser," but he'd called me wonderful. I couldn't throw his compliment back in his face. "I don't know. I didn't want you involved. This is my mess. I . . . You're an evangelist and I have a gun."

"I have a gun."

"But you need one for your business. I have a gun because I'm contemplating shooting off a pinky toe."

Powers laughed a deep, throaty sound that said I'd just helped him release a load of stress. "Can you even work that thing?"

"I had two four-hour lessons at Shooter's Galaxy. I'm a pro."

He laughed again and then his voice took on a serious tone. "Tamera, please come home. Let me help you handle this the right way."

"You said Leon was spending money like a fool. I've seen him. He is. He'll be broke by Friday. I . . . can't. I've got to at least try to reason with him . . . to get some of the money back."

"Tamera."

I closed my eyes to his plea, but I struggled with closing my heart. "I appreciate all you've done for me. I really do, but I've got to do this. I've come this far. A conversation with Leon isn't going to hurt."

"But you could get hurt. You may not be the only person with a gun."

"I have the element of surprise on my side. I promise. I won't let him hurt me. I have a plan."

We were silent for a long time. I knew Powers was thinking. He was trying to find the words to convince me that I was making a mistake. I also knew I was new at this. I knew this wasn't television. It wasn't a Hollywood movie like *Mr. and Mrs. Smith*. I wasn't Angelina Jolie. But this was my life. This missing money was my problem. I had to solve it my way, so I wasn't going to be talked out of getting it.

"Wait for me," Powers begged. "Let's talk through the plan when I get there."

"No." I shook my head. "I'm breaking the law. Man's and God's. I don't want to involve you. I'll be home by early afternoon, and I promise I'll tell you all about it when I get there. Money or no money, okay?"

He was silent. It was not okay. "Wish me luck, or better yet, say a prayer for me. I know God is listening to you." I hung up the phone.

Chapter Fifteen

It was eight o'clock in the morning. I knew those partyin', spendin', thievin' ballers would definitely still be in bed. I knocked on the door three times before I finally heard a woman's voice on the other side. "Who the heck is it?"

"Hotel services, ma'am." I disguised my voice.

"Yeah, well service something else. The 'do not disturb' sign is up and it's eight—" I thought Delilah wasn't going to open up, but as she was complaining the door was opening.

As soon as I got a glimpse of the little tart, I pushed it hard, throwing Delilah's barely clothed form onto the floor. She screamed. I stepped in and pulled out the gun. "Shut up! Or I'll put a bullet in you."

Delilah sniffled and crawled back to the bed where Leon was sprawled out naked as the day he was born and knocked out cold. Seeing him like that sickened me and fueled my anger. I realized now wasn't the time to get emotional. I pointed the gun at Delilah. "On your feet, tramp, and wake that lowlife up."

Delilah scampered to Leon's side and began to poke him in the head. "Leon, Leon, it's your wife."

"Oh, so you know who I am." Our eyes met and Delilah started sobbing. I fought the urge to shoot her.

Leon's eyes popped open. It took him a moment to come out of his sleepy haze, but when he did and he recognized me, shock and fear were all over his face. He cursed.

"I'm here for the money." I raised the gun to show him I meant business.

Leon pulled his body up on the bed and attempted to reach over the side of it.

"Don't move. I'll shoot."

"I'm just trying to get my drawers."

"I've seen your pitiful behind naked before. Remember, I'm your wife." There was a man's satin robe at the foot of the bed. I motioned toward it. "Give that to him," I ordered Delilah.

Her face was marred with a permanent grimace of fear. She looked like one of those distorted characters etched into the walls of the house of horrors at the amusement park. She followed my instructions and Leon attempted to cover himself like he thought I might shoot him in the family jewels.

"Tammy, I . . . I . . . know you kind of mad wit' me, but a gun . . . Wha . . . what . . . what . . . ch . . . ch . . . choo doing with a gun?"

Stuttering. What happened to his good diction? "I'm doing what you did. Robbing my spouse blind, honey. But I don't have five months to wine and dine you. I don't have time to listen to your sob stories or hear about your dreams, so I figured a semi-automatic handgun would get me what I wanted a whole lot faster."

"Leon!" Delilah's breaths came heavy like she was having some kind of panic attack.

"Shut up, baby." Leon silenced her as he threw his legs over the side of the bed and stood. "Tam, you really need to stop pointing that gun at us. You don't know how to use that thing. You might hurt somebody."

"Not somebody." I stepped closer to the bed. "You."

Leon's hand trembled a bit. I could tell he was trying to think of something to say. "Tamera, I think we should be able to talk about this without that gun."

"Really?" I asked, shaking my head. "I don't remember you talking to me before you stole my money."

Leon sighed.

"I would ask you the question most people ask in this situation. You know, how could you? But I had you checked out, Leon, or is it Larry or Luther or Lex?" His eyes widened when I threw his aliases at him. "I won't ask, because I already know how you could. You're a thief and a con artist and so is your bad weave–wearing friend."

"Excuse me." Delilah rolled her neck.

I shook my head. "Save it, sweetheart. The first thing you should have done when he gave you some money was fly to Atlanta and get yourself a decent piece of hair."

Delilah cut her eyes at me and raised her hand to pat the matted mess she'd obviously not tied up last night. She mumbled something under her breath, but I didn't hear it because my phone rang. I pulled it out of my jacket pocket and recognized Powers's cell number. I ignored it. It began to ring again and then there was a loud knock on the door. I jumped. So did Leon and Delilah. "Who's that?" I asked.

They both shrugged like dumb and dumber. There was another knock and then a voice on the other side of the door that was faint, but discernible. "Tamera, it's me, Powers. Open up."

No way. I rolled my eyes upward and let out a long sigh. *No, he is not here.* I bit my lip. "Don't either one of you move, or, I swear, I'll shoot and then you'll know I know how to use this thing." I slowly closed the distance between where I'd been and the door. I made sure to keep the gun trained on my captives while I turned the doorknob with my free hand, but Leon leapt across the edge of the bed. He startled me so bad, I screamed and dropped the gun. The door flew open, and Powers entered the room. Seeing a half-naked Leon running in a silk robe must have turned on his cop instincts, because with lightening speed he charged at Leon, knocking him to the ground. I noticed Delilah had inched a few feet in our direction. I caught her eye as she looked from me to the floor. That tramp was going for the gun. I was closer, so I rushed to it and aimed it in her direction. She backed up.

This was getting out of control. I kicked Leon in the lower back so hard that I felt his bone through my tennis shoe. Powers gained the upper hand and cracked Leon in the jaw. Leon whined like a puppy with a foot on his tail.

Powers got up off the floor. "Nice work."

"Thanks. I was making progress before you arrived."

"I can see that, but I thought you might need some help staying out of jail, so I took the first flight I could get."

My stomach fluttered. He was rushing to my rescue. *How sweet.* No one had ever done that before.

"Hey," Leon barked, getting up off the floor. He was holding his jaw. "You mind telling me who this is?" He sounded like a jealous husband.

"It's my partner in crime. Why should you get to have all the fun?" I twisted my lips into a shy smile and winked at Powers.

Leon pulled his robe together and returned to his spot against the wall with Delilah. I heard her whisper, "I thought you said she was stupid."

I moved closer to the bed. Trained the gun on Leon. "Stupid?"

He stepped back, shook his head, and gritted his teeth. "Dee, keep your friggin' mouth closed."

Delilah threw her hands up. "I'm just saying, she over there and we over here. She don't look very stupid to me, Leon!"

"Shut up!" I yelled. "Put your hands up." They did.

Powers took a few steps closer. "May I?" He questioned me with his eyes. I nodded and Powers took over. "Leon, you know why Tamera's here. She wants the money. Now she had a couple hours in a shooting range, but I'm not sure she's good enough to not accidentally fire off a round. The longer she holds that gun in her hand, the more likely she is to kill one of you. So, where is it?"

"I ain't answering you. I still don't even know who you are." Leon put his hands down and Delilah followed suit. "Tamera ain't 'bout to shoot nobody."

I reached into my pocket and pulled out the silencer. I had it on the gun so fast I surprised myself. I pointed the barrel down at the mattress, near Leon, and fired. Everybody in the room jumped, including me. Leon began to pee. I pressed my lips together to keep from laughing.

"She could kill both of you and nobody would even hear it," Powers said.

Leon looked down at his wet leg and shook his head. "Lord have mercy, girl. It's in an account. I got the paperwork right here in the safe."

"Leon!" Delilah put her hands on her hips and shot daggers at him with her eyes. "What are you doing?"

"I ain't dying up in here over no money." Leon moved to the room safe and began to open it.

"Hold up." Powers stopped him. I remembered Powers warning me that I might not be the only one who had a gun, and realized if Leon was packing, the safe would be the place to keep his weapon.

Leon stepped aside for Powers to get at the safe and, with reluctance, recited the code.

Delilah was incensed. "Wait a minute. You can't hand it all over. It's not *just* your money."

I couldn't believe this woman. I wanted to shoot her for having the nerve to think my money was now hers. "Shut up, trick!" I raised the gun at her. "These bullets ain't marital property."

Delilah rolled her eyes and let her body fall to the ground like an angry child having a temper tantrum. Within seconds the safe was emptied.

Powers tossed a wad of cash on the bed. "This is about five thousand dollars." Then he pulled out Leon's precious prized jersey case and some paperwork. He scanned it, and then looked at me. "Fifty thousand dollars in an account in the Cayman Islands."

My heart sank. $50,000 of it wasn't even in the country. I dropped into a nearby chair. It never occurred to me that he'd send it offshore. Powers seemed to know what I was thinking. He picked up the $5,000 and rushed to my side, kneeling. "This is good, Tamera. It makes things easier. We can just have him wire the money to your bank account."

I looked up at Leon, who was rolling his eyes. Delilah had her arms crossed over her chest. She was leering up at Leon, disgusted with him.

Powers stood. "Mr. Watson, we've got some banking to do. Where's your laptop?"

Leon groaned.

Chapter Sixteen

Powers and Leon hovered around the laptop for a while. I provided the number for a credit union account I had through my job and within ten minutes of them completing the transaction I called and verified the funds were there. I put the five in my duffel bag. *$55,000.* Things were looking up, but not quite up enough. "I want the rest." The gun that had been at my side was now pointing at Leon again.

Leon shrugged his shoulders nonchalantly. "That's it. I got a Mercedes coupe in the garage, this room, and, shoot, I done spent 'bout twenty thousand since we got here." He took a money clip off the table and tossed it to me. "There's two thousand dollars." He went and pulled money out of Delilah's handbag. She hissed like a rattlesnake. He tossed a wad of cash on the bed. "That's about a thousand."

Leon shrugged again. I smiled slyly. "You do think I'm stupid. I know you spent some, but there's money in a safe deposit account at New State Bank." Leon's eyes bugged wide. "Now, hubby, I want you to tie that tramp up and tape her mouth with this." I removed a roll of duct tape from my bag and tossed it on the bed. "Put your clothes on. We're going to get the rest of my money."

Delilah was all over him. "Leon, I know you not going to—"

"Dee, I done told you to shut up! What you want me to do, take a bullet so you can have the money?"

Delilah continued to rant. "I waited patiently while you was working this deal. If you give her—"

I was sick of the bickering back and forth. I put another bullet in the mattress.

"Tamera, stop." I felt Powers's strong hand on my shoulder. It traveled the length of my arm to the gun. I looked at him out of my peripheral vision. "The only way to get that money is to force him at gunpoint to the bank. You can't do that."

"Yes, I can."

"No, you can't."

"That fifty-eight thousand is not even enough to cover the corporate money I have to return. And what about the money I spent finding him, and my grandmother's house? I have a building. I have plans. I need the rest of it. I can't let them have the money from my grandmother's house."

"The key to the box isn't here. It's probably in the hotel safe in the lobby, but even if we had it, you can't walk down the street holding a gun in his back." Powers took my free hand and turned me in Leon and Delilah's direction. "Look at them. They aren't even worth what you'd have to go through when this all went bad."

I broke down and started crying. He was right. I wanted the money so bad, I wasn't thinking. If Leon did one crazy thing on the street, I'd have to shoot him. I couldn't shoot him, in public or private. I wasn't a murderer. It would never work. I handed Powers the gun and he reached up and wiped the tears from my face with his thumb. "I'll tell you what we can do though." Powers careened his neck in Leon's direction. "We'll take the paperwork for that Mercedes." He paused and smiled slyly. "And that Michael Jordan jersey."

Delilah let her body fall to the floor. "Leon!" Her whine was music to my ears.

Leon threw his arms up in disgust and started shaking his head. "Who is this dude?"

I grabbed Powers around the neck with so much force that I almost toppled him over. *Who is he?* "Super Powers," I whispered in his ear. I squeezed him tight and stepped back. "I would never have thought of the car."

Powers winked and flashed me a hundred-watt smile. "I told you to wait for me."

Chapter Seventeen

I stood with the rest of the congregation and gave my girl a hardy hand clap for her rendition of "Is Your All on the Altar." Those voice lessons were turning her into the next Karen Clark Sheard. She brought down the house and, more importantly, she moved my spirit. I needed the message Pastor preached today and I needed that song.

I milled around and spoke to some of the members as I waited. Everyone knew my plans for The Micah Center were on hold. They also knew my husband was gone, and while there was some whispering, most were sympathetic and encouraging. "Hold on to God's unchanging hand. He'll make a way for that center to open." Words like that. They did my heart good and gave me hope.

Erin and the rest of the choir poured out of a back room. They were still giving my girl high fives and pats on the back. I was proud of her. She made her way to where I was standing. "I felt like you sang that song just for me." I gave her a tight squeeze around the neck. "I got an application for Sunday's Best in the car."

Erin waved a hand. "Girl, that was nothing. Just a little somethin'. I still haven't shown y'all folks how blessedly talented a sista is."

We laughed and walked out of the sanctuary.

"I have two-for-one coupons for brunch today. Linda—you know, the chick with the Angela Davis afro who we had to put on the last row in the choir loft so she wouldn't block everybody with her hair?"

I nodded, amused at Erin's colorful description.

"She got engaged Friday night and I heard the ring was something else. He did some big deal proposal on some cable station that nobody watches, but she's going to tell us the details today. Come on and celebrate with us. It'll do you good to socialize."

I shook my head. I couldn't help but think about how long I'd waited to find Mr. Right and now less than a year later I was right back where I started. Alone. "You tell me all about it later. I can't do brunch today."

Erin sunk visibly. "Come on. It's been forever since you joined us. I know you not still trying to hide your face. Don't nobody care about Leon."

I shook my head again. "There's something I have to do. I already made arrangements with Timothy House. They're coming to pick up the boxes in the morning."

Erin instantly knew what I meant. Timothy was a transitional house for homeless men who were getting back on their feet.

"You want some help?"

"No, this is something I have to do by myself. It's way overdue."

Erin gave me a tight squeeze. "I love you, girl."

I squeezed back. "Love you too." I let her go and climbed into my car to pack up the last reminders of Leon Watson.

Leon's belongings filled six large cartons. My legs were tired from going up and down the stairs. I wished I could just throw it all out the back window and light a match, but the men in the Timothy House needed these clothes. The stuff Leon left behind that was a curse to me would be a blessing to them.

Once the closet was empty, I moved everything near the front door and went back upstairs to vacuum and dust. An hour later I was finished. My bedroom looked like it had before I had gotten married, except for the unisex bedding and drapes. Maybe I would pull my lavender floral comforter set back out of storage and girly the place up again.

The doorbell rang. I bounced off the bed and jogged down the stairs. I wasn't expecting anyone and I'd taken to making sure to check at all times just in case Leon decided to pay me a visit, so I looked out the peephole before I opened the door. My heart leapt.

"I was in the neighborhood. I thought I'd stop by and check on you." I moved back and allowed Powers to enter. He looked at the boxes suspiciously. "Moving?"

"Moving someone out." I smiled and we both stared at each other for a moment. My heart was racing a mile a minute. I was so glad to see him. "I have homemade lemonade. Would you like some?"

He nodded and followed me into the kitchen, where I washed my hands and poured two glasses. We took seats at the table.

"How are you?"

I nodded. "I'm good. Really, really good."

"Have you heard from Leon?"

"Not a word. I'm sure he and Delilah have figured out some new scam. He's moved on. He won't bother me."

"I agree." Powers took a sip. "The alarm code for the house and the locks?"

"Changed." I took a deep breath. "I also filed for an annulment."

His eyes met mine and we held our gazes for a while. "That's for the best. The sooner you're free of him, the sooner you can move on with your life."

"I haven't given up on my dream." I paused. "I'm still going to open the center one day. I returned the corporate funds. Thanks to you, I have almost twenty thousand dollars leftover. I'm so glad you thought about the car or I'd still owe people money. I got the matching corporate monies once. I know I can get them again."

"I'm just glad you're okay."

Our eyes locked again and I realized I knew very little about this man who was making my heart thud. But I did know one very important thing. He'd helped me get my life back, helped me save my dignity, and that was worth more than any amount of money.

"I'm glad to hear you're not giving up, because I actually have some good news." Powers removed an envelope from his pocket.

I raised my eyebrows. "I could use good news. What is it?"

"Well, you know I was digging around in Leon's past. It turns out he has money in an unclaimed fund that he apparently doesn't know anything about."

I sat up straighter. "Are you kidding?"

"He had a great aunt who died more than ten years ago in Mississippi. She owned a house. It wasn't worth much. The value of it had been depreciating every year. The county tore it down to build a school and put the money from the settlement offer in unclaimed funds. Guess who her only living heir is?"

I shook my head and chuckled. "No way."

Powers nodded. "It's almost fifteen thousand dollars. Once the civil claim against Leon is filed, you can put a lien on that money. He doesn't even know about it to fight it." Powers slid the envelope to me. I reached for it and my fingers grazed his. The tingle was so electric it sent a shock through my entire body. Powers must have felt it too, because he reached for my hand

and intertwined his fingers with mine. "So you still have a little over twenty thousand, this fifteen, and, I've been thinking. I'd like to invest in a dream." His mouth broke into that incredibly sexy, crooked smile I'd come to love.

"You are such a superpower." We met each other halfway across the table and finally kissed.

Best Served Cold

E.N. Joy

Prologue

Social Networking: The Start of the
End of a Relationship

I'm sitting here at my laptop sweating like a lying and cheating husband whose wife just force-fed him a truth serum. It's funny I should use that type of comparison, considering it was all of my husband's lies, evasiveness, and lies by omission that have me in the position I'm in right now.

I never imagined that at forty years old I would be doing things with my husband that I did at twenty-five. On the count of three, all minds out the gutter, because that is not what I'm talking about. One, two, three.

Don't get me wrong, my husband and I met around my mid-twenties. I remember quite well some of the things we used to do. He wasn't my husband back then, though, and God knows I was nowhere near saved or else I probably wouldn't have done half the things I did with that man. Now look who needs to get their mind out of the gutter.

Anyway, it's not those things I'm referring to. I'm talking about this: what I'm doing now, what I've done for the last couple of days, and what I'm about to do.

What I'm about to do will change everyone's perception of my husband for the worse. His brothers and sisters, his mother and father, coworkers, friends and church family will all get to see him for who he really is and not what he makes himself out to be. Everybody always puts him on this pedestal and he just eats it up. They have him thinking he's God's gift to the world. Maybe he's not God's gift to the world, but I at least thought he was God's gift to me. But God's gifts come without sorrow, so how could that be when my relationship with my husband has left me the epitome of sorrow?

Nobody placed my husband on a higher pedestal than I did. I promise you I would have bet my life that that man walked on water. After the Father, the Son, and the Holy Spirit, Lee Royce Hampton was the best thing that could have ever happened to me. He was a hard worker with an honest career, a provider for myself and our two children. He never put his hands on me in a violent manner and neither did he abuse drugs or alcohol. In fact, he was a man of God who was brought up in the church—strayed momentarily—but when he went back he took me with him and introduced me to Jesus. What woman wouldn't fall head over heels in love with a man who introduced her to Jesus Christ Himself?

In addition to all those other things, my man came home to me every night. Whenever I called him, he picked up his phone. Whenever his phone rang when he was with me, he answered it. Of course, that hadn't always been the case, which takes me back to when I was twenty-five and had first met him. It was around 1997. Everything was all good for the first few months of our relationship, but that's because we were both starting up new careers and very involved with our jobs. We didn't spend a great deal of time together, but the time we did spend together was always quality.

For the next couple of months after that, once we were pretty much settled into our new positions at work and our new position in each other's lives, we started spending more time together. That's when I noticed that the more time we spent together, the more his pager would end up on vibrate.

"When I'm with you, I just want to focus on you. I don't want my pager always going off and stuff." That was the reply Lee had given me when I questioned him about the continuous vibration in his pocket. He'd pull it out and acknowledge it, but then would place it back in his pocket without ever calling anybody back.

"Okay," I had replied with a smile on my face, all the while waiting for the opportunity to get my hands on that pager. I mean, did he really think I had bought that excuse? Well, if he had at that moment, two days later he hadn't. I was at his apartment and he was preparing a meal when he realized he was out of an ingredient.

"I have to run to the store right quick. I'll be back in a jiff," he said while running out with keys in hand, but leaving his pager right smack on his living room table.

"Bingo!" I shouted, picking up the now very much outdated device. "God is good all the time, and all the time God is good." And like I mentioned before, I wasn't even saved back then, but I still knew who to give thanks to. It could have only been a miracle of God that could lead a man to leave his pager behind when he knows darn well he's up to no good. And no good is just what Lee had been up to.

I went through his pager and found all kinds of numbers and codes; stuff like the "Hello" and the "I Miss You" symbols. I knew these were from women because dudes didn't do that kind of stuff with each other.

Being the amateur sleuth that I was, I immediately headed to his nightstand drawer because I knew what I was looking for would be there. And so it was; Lee's address book. I looked through the address book and matched up some of the numbers in the address book with some of the numbers in his pager. Just like I had thought, they all pretty much belonged to women. I recognized some of the names as chicks he had mentioned "kickin' it with" in the past. So if they were the past, then why were their numbers still in his pager? If they were in the past, then why had a couple of them paged him as recently as earlier that day? *Because he was a liar,* that's why.

I figured if he'd lied about that, what else had he lied about? I pouted my way back into the living room and flopped down on the couch in disgust.

All of a sudden there was this flashing light going off. No, not in my head, but on the phone resting on his end table.

"What the heck?" I said as I made my way over to the phone. I looked down at the caller ID screen and, lo and behold, one of the female's names I'd just seen in his address book was streaming across the caller ID screen. Cell phones might not have been popular then, but caller ID was. A call was coming in, but the phone wasn't ringing, just lights flashing. I picked the entire phone up, the base and all, without picking up the receiver. I quickly discovered that the ringer had been turned off.

So not only was this fool putting his pager on vibrate when he was around me, but he was turning off the ringer to his land line when he had me over.

"Wow! Really, Lee?" That wasn't a popular saying back then, but that's what I would have said if it had been. And that's what I would have said had I been saved. But it wasn't and I wasn't, so those were not quite the words that flew out of my mouth.

I was enraged and not feeling myself anymore, so much so that before I knew it, this word was flying out of my mouth too: "Hello."

Yep, I had gone and answered that man's phone.

"Hello," I repeated, agitated when the caller failed to reply to my first greeting.

"Uh, hello, is Lee home?" the timid-sounding female asked after hesitating.

"No, he's out at the store picking up something so he can finish up the dinner he's making me." I know I was wrong, dead wrong, but remember I was in my twenties and I wasn't saved. See, that's the very reason why I know I could never run for president. Being unsaved in my twenties would never be able to stand up to the scrutiny presidential candidates are subjected to. I mean, thank God there wasn't YouTube and all that stuff back then to prove a lot of what I might be accused of, but still, I'm sure somebody has old pictures and VHS tapes that could have me out of the presidential race quicker than Herman Cain.

"Oh, at the store?" she questioned as if she hadn't heard me clearly the first time. Still I obliged her.

"Yep, he's at the store."

"Oh, okay." She paused. I gave her all the time she needed to gather her words, because I knew she still had more to say.

"Is this his sister?"

That was logical for her to ask, considering he had two sisters.

"Nope." I was short. She paused. Again, I gave her all the time she needed to gather her words, because, yet and still, I knew she had more to say; I would have.

"Are you someone he's seeing?" I guess she decided not to beat around the bush anymore by questioning whether or not I was a cousin, aunt, mother, housekeeper, et cetera. . . .

"Yes, I am. As a matter of fact, I'm someone he's been seeing for several months now. And you are?"

She didn't pause this time. She was more than ready for my query as she immediately replied, "I'm someone whose house he just left."

Now it was me who had room for pause. My brain started churning. When I'd first arrived at Lee's apartment that evening, he wasn't there. I had to sit out in my car for a few minutes and wait for him to get home. Once he arrived he'd apologized and blamed work for his tardiness, but now here Miss Thing was stating otherwise.

"Then if he just left your house, then you know he's not here, right? He's probably still driving, huh?" Before she could respond I continued. "Is there a message I can give him? Although he might not be able to return your call until after he finishes making me dinner." I let out a mischievous chuckle. "Make that after I give him dessert."

She paused, but this time it wasn't to gather her words. She had no more. "No, no message." It was a wrap. I'd gotten the "W."

The line went dead and even though I had the victory over her, I was seeing red.

"That lying son of a . . ." Now how many times do I have to reiterate that I was not yet saved? *Hallelu-jerrrrr*.

I slammed that phone down and made a beeline to his bedroom. I started rummaging through his stuff like a wild woman. I wasn't looking for anything in particular this time, just good old-fashioned proof. I was hoping to stumble upon an earring, panties, cards, love notes—proof of just how many women Mr. Lee was entertaining besides me.

I couldn't have cared less about being caught by him returning home. As a matter of fact, even when I heard him enter the apartment I continued my search. By now I had completed my search in his bedroom and was slinging the pillows off of his living room couch and digging down in it to see what remnants of another chick I could find.

"Musik, what on earth are you doing?" Lee had said to me, entering the apartment with a grocery bag in hand.

"I think the question is what are you doing?" I snapped, picking his pager up off the table and then throwing it at him. Thank God that boy was fast and was able to duck quickly; otherwise, that pager would have split his wig in two. I was on some *Kill Bill*-ish.

Because now that fifteen years later I am saved, I can't repeat the rest of my conversation with Lee. The devil himself would have to edit it if he tried to tell it. But what I will say is that Lee and I addressed the situation up until the wee hours of the morning. When all was said and done we'd agreed that we were exclusive and that me having male "friends" and him having female "friends" we'd had past relationships with or had slept with was out of the question. We were officially exclusive. Funny thing was, I, being a woman, had already assumed we were exclusive. After all, I didn't have any male "friends."

Once I'd met Lee and knew that he was "the one" I had cut every guy off I had been dating. I mean, I had literally sat by my phone with my address book in hand making calls, ending any type of relationship with the male of the species whatsoever. For some reason I thought the feeling had been mutual and that Lee had done the same. I had settled for better late than never because he had done it that night.

After that episode, I had vowed to never act that way over a man again. I managed to keep that vow for fifteen years, too. But then technology changed and there was more to contend with than breaking into pagers, address books, caller ID, and searching for love letters and cards. Now we have cell phones. And if that isn't bad enough, some college kid had to come along and make things even harder on women by coming up with some social network site called www.FaceIt.com.

I'd seen on the news once that FaceIt.com had been cited in thirty percent of divorce filings. I never imagined I might become part of that percentage. But will it soon be my reality? What I found after breaking into Lee's FaceIt page broke my heart. It was now sending me on a much worse warpath than I'd gone on back when I was twenty-five. After all, Lee was just my boyfriend back then. There were no kids involved and no vows. But now I am his wife. Now there are two kids involved. Dang it, there are vows.

Back then I was just out to find proof and confront Lee with it. Now I had found my proof, and instead of just confronting Lee with it, I want to destroy him with it. With the push of just one button that is exactly what is about to go down. I'm about to forward and post information I found on his FaceIt page that will put his lying, cheating self on blast. With just the push of one button, I'm about to reveal to the world who the real Lee is. On the count of three, Lee is going to suffer the same pain and humiliation I'm feeling. The pain and humiliation he was causing me.

One, two . . .

Chapter One

Love at Second Sight

"Excuse me, don't I know you from somewhere?" Those were the first words Lee said to me all those years ago.

As fine as this chocolate specimen of a man was, at the time I wondered if this dude could have come up with a better line than that? *Cats still use this line? As a matter of fact, why would anyone ever want to use that line in the first place?* I'd thought. As crude as it may have been of me, and as fine as Lee was, I laughed in his face and continued pushing my cart up the Kroger grocery store aisle.

He himself couldn't help but join me in my laughter. "That did sound kind of corny, huh?" He smiled.

Okay, so why did he have the most straight, almost bone-white teeth I'd ever seen? I promise on the moon I saw those little ding flashy things flashing on his teeth. The ones they show on cartoons in order to exaggerate the whiteness of someone's teeth. They practically blinded me.

"Corny is not the word," I told him, his smile causing me to smile.

"But for real though, I did see you the other day when you were out."

I couldn't believe he was going to insist on riding that line out. I crossed my arms and turned to him, still smiling, all the while thinking, *Ohhh, I want to do him.* And just let me clarify that saved or unsaved, sinner or saint, that thought would have still been on my mind. I'm not trying to offend anyone, just keepin' it real. Or should I say, "Telling the truth and shaming the devil." Keepin' it one hunnid, though, there was no shame in my game that I was about to play with him, a man who hadn't yet told me his name. But I wanted to play nonetheless. Hey, a kid knows how much fun a toy potentially has just by looking at it. And I was looking, at him, up and down. I was checking him out from head to toe, but somewhat discretely and with a smile on my lips and in my eyes.

Not a single saved sister in the church today could have blamed me either. Half of them prayed every day that God would place a man like this at their feet. Yet He'd chosen to place him at mine, a chick who only called on Jesus when she stubbed her toe.

"So you saw me when I was out the other day?" My words were laced with disbelief. "And just where was it I was at?"

"Satin Saturday's. The Ohio Expo Center." He leaned into my ear, his lips close, but not touching my flesh. "And you were killin' 'em in that gold and cream floor-length dress. I mean, lady, you were crucial."

I could feel his breath on my lobe. All of a sudden I had goosies running up and down my arms. I felt him pull away and it was in slow motion. My eyes looked up and locked with his. He winked.

It took me a minute to find my voice. I think it was lost in his eyes. But eventually I did. "I guess I stand corrected, so you do know me from somewhere." It hadn't been a corny line after all. It had been the truth.

"And now I'd just like to get to know you . . ." He paused, gave me the once-over, and then finished with, " . . . better."

Girl, don't you let that Kool-Aid Man come crashing out your mouth, I scolded myself, feeling a huge Kool-Aid grin coming on. I immediately got my emotions intact. I could not let this guy know that he had me feeling a certain kind of way after not even five minutes of walking into my life.

"And tell me, Mr. . . . ."

"Lee," he filled in the blank. "Lee Royce Hampton."

"Oh, you goin' full name on me." I chuckled.

"Oh, my bad." He put his head down and tried to wipe his grin away with his hand. "I guess I'm just used to my moms always calling me by my full name." He looked back up at me. Was this boy blushing?

"Well, my mama only called me by my full name when I was in trouble. So if you're used to your mama always calling you by your full name, that must mean only one thing: that you're trouble."

"Naw, not me." He turned away from me again. Yes, he was blushing. I was making a grown man blush. And that was rated G versus what he was making me do.

I decided to take the conversation back to where I wanted it to be. "So, Mr. Lee Royce Hampton, just how do you plan on getting to know me better?"

"Well, I'd like to start by getting your phone number. Next, maybe we can engage in hopefully some decent conversation, then maybe go out to spend some time together to see how we connect."

Connect? Musik, girl, get your mind out of the gutter. This man could be husband material. I could ruin everything if I were to be too open. *Open? Stop it.* Talk about the mind being a battlefield. This seemed to be a losing battle.

"You look good." *Did I say that? Did he hear me say that?*

"Excuse me?"

"That sounds good."

"Oh, cool."

Whew. There is a God.

"So how about you write down my number and call me when you get a minute, then I'll let you finish getting your little"—he looked in my cart—"Frosted Flakes, grapes, Mike Sells potato chips . . . ?"

We shared a laugh.

"Okay. Sounds good." Who was I kidding? It sounded *greeaaatttt!* I was just quoting Tony the Tiger from my box of Frosted Flakes.

I used my grocery list and the pen I had been using to cross out items as I placed them in my cart to write down his phone number. "So when's a good time to call you?"

"With you, it's all good." He hit me with a head nod.

Dang this boy was smooth.

"So, I'm going to head on home . . . and go sit and wait by the phone. I'm expecting an important phone call." He pulled out his car keys and went to walk away.

Noticing he didn't have a grocery cart, basket, or not even a pack of crackers in his hands I called out to him. "Hey, but don't you have to do your grocery shopping first?"

"Nahhh," he said nonchalantly over his shoulder and kept walking. "I already got everything I need."

He had me. He knew he had me and in more ways than one.

We'd met on a Monday in the grocery store and I called him on Wednesday, even though I so badly had wanted to call him the same day I met him. I wanted to call him the next day even, but my girl, Trina, said that would make me look desperate. Dang, just *looking* desperate—I was desperate.

Just so there is no confusion, let me clarify that I wasn't desperate for a man. I had guys I was seeing, dating, just kickin' it with, just friends with or whatever people call it. So the company of the male of the species was not an area in which I was lacking. What I was lacking was the kind of instant connection, that fire, chemistry, attraction I had with Lee. None of the other guys could do that for me. None of them had done that for me. That's what I had been desperate for—the infamous fairytale. And if every woman on the planet was to be honest, she'd admit that she, too, desired the fairytale.

We want that "love at first sight" thing. We want indescribable chemistry. We want that man who made us feel like we were the only woman in the world. From the first moment I saw Lee, I just felt that he could be the leading man in every fairytale I'd ever seen, heard, or read. Only this time it would be my fairytale . . . come true.

After three days of talking on the phone, getting to know the basics about one another, Lee finally asked me out. It was a Friday when he asked me out for a date that following day, a Saturday.

"I'll pick you up at ten-thirty," he said after I agreed to go out with him.

"Ten-thirty? Dude, you might as well wait until midnight and make it an official booty call." I was a little offended.

He laughed. I failed to see the humor.

"Ten-thirty in the morning," he clarified.

"Oh," I said, feeling a little stupid for jumping to the conclusion that he just wanted to bed me without even having the decency to bread me. Bread and Bed is when a man at least spends some money—dough, bread—on a chick, or breaks bread with her—buys her a meal—

before he tries to get some. Not that I was the type of
girl who lowered myself to those standards . . . all the
time. Hey, just being honest here. Don't judge me.

"So, is ten-thirty in the A.M. okay?" he asked.

"Yes, sure," I replied. "It's a date."

We ended the call and I immediately ran to my closet
to start figuring out what I was going to wear.

"Dang, I should have asked him where we were going," I realized, clueless as to how I should dress. I
assumed he must have been taking me to breakfast.
Where else could we possibly be going at ten-thirty in
the morning? After picking out my outfit I immediately
got on my treadmill and then did crunches. It was as
if I could lose the ten pounds I had been telling myself
for months I was going to lose prior to my date the next
day. After an hour on the tread and several ridiculous
sets of crunches, I came to the conclusion that I'd have
no such luck and decided to settle in for the night . . .
with a pizza from Domino's. Hey, I'd eat a light breakfast.

The next morning I was ready for my official first
date with Lee. It was mid-July in Reynoldsburg, Ohio,
so even at ten-thirty in the morning it was warm
enough for me to rock my strapless sundress. It was a
little short for what I'd normally wear, but I knew I just
had to have it from the moment I saw that model wearing it in the catalog I ordered it from. It was the perfect
dress to show off the tattoo of a black butterfly I had on
my left shoulder. I'd gotten it done on a trip to Atlanta
with Trina and a couple of my other girls. It was done
by the same tattoo artist who did Tupac's BALLIN tattoo.

I decided on some gold metallic sandals that matched
perfectly with my oversized gold hoop earrings and my
knockoff Versace bag I'd bought in New York. Being
five foot and nine inches tall, I felt modelistic to say

the least. My naturally curly hair rested on my brown-skinned shoulders. I had my hair pushed back with a pair of Versace shades I'd picked up in Vegas. Those were real.

At first I decided to go light on the makeup, figuring, *it's just a morning breakfast. It's not like we're going out to a club or anything.* But then I thought about the fact that Lee might want to spend the entire day with me. What if we went to a movie or something afterward or over one of his friend's house? I decided to go a little bit heavier on the makeup, even using my mascara to blot on a fake Marilyn Monroe sexy mole above my upper lip.

"Purrrrrrr," I teased myself, clawing the mirror like Catwoman. It was on and poppin'!

My phone rang just as I put my makeup away. "Hello," I answered.

"Music to my ears, literally." Lee's voice took morning glory to a whole new meaning.

"Good morning, sir," I cheesed through the phone.

"I love the sound of your smile."

How did he know? I had to pull the phone away from my ear and look at it. Could he see this big smile on my face through the phone?

"Hey, I just pulled up in your driveway," he informed me.

"Oh, and you didn't get lost." I was impressed.

"You gave me good directions."

"I love a man who knows how to take good direction."

"I love a woman who knows how to give them."

"Don't you think we're just a tad bit too early in this relationship to be using the L word?" I teased.

"When it's love at first sight, it's love at first sight," I joked. "I guess in your case, though, it would have to be love at second sight, considering you saw me once at Satin Saturday's and then a second time at Kroger."

"Hmmm, I thought we were on even playing grounds," Lee said. "I'm almost certain you saw me that Saturday too. Or do you always speak to strangers?"

He had me stumped. No way had I spoken to that man and didn't try to take it a step further. Then it hit me like a ton of bricks. "You're the guy in the red suit who Trina said I was going to kick myself for blowing off."

"I don't know about all that. But I do remember the moment you stepped through the doors and walked in the place. I waved and said 'hello.' You—"

"Had to pee like a race horse and dashed right by you, giving you nothing more than a wave and a 'Hey.'" I remembered it clearly now. Only he was a blur. All I could recall seeing was dark skin, a blur of red, and a hand waving. I heard someone greet me and figured it was the blur in the red suit.

I'd held my pee in that long line to get inside Satin Saturday's and thought I was going to bust if I didn't run straight to the toilet. After I'd finished my business and come out of the stall to wash my hands, all I remember Trina saying was:

"Girl, are you crazy? How you just gon' blow off the finest guy up in this place? In the city? He must not be from here, because Lord knows I would have remembered seeing his fine self before. Girl, you better dry your hands and go out there, repent—to him, the Lord, or whoever it takes—and get his number." Trina was talking a mile a minute like her life depended on it.

"Heck, why don't you go out there and get him if it's like that?" I replied, drying my hands.

"'Cause it's you he wants, not me." She hit me on the shoulder. *"Did you see the way he said hello to you?*

It was like you were the only woman up in here. Like you were the only woman in the world. Musik, you said as soon as you meet Mr. Right you were going to settle down, get married, and have babies. Well, your Mr. Right is right out there. Right now. So go, go, go!"

Trina practically pushed me out of the bathroom door with her melodramatic self. She brushed by me, snatching up my hand, and dragging me back over near the entrance where the red blur once was.

I heard Trina's heels screech, nearly peeling off the wood from the floor. "He's gone. He's gone."

I thought she was about to cry. I couldn't help but laugh. "T, it's not that serious."

"Oh, but it was." After a couple of seconds her frown turned upside down. "Hey, the night's still young. We have plenty of time to find him." Once again she yanked my hand. I put all my weight down and kept her from pulling me another step.

"Look, I came here to kick it and have fun, not hunt down some strange dude. I ain't all that, but I look good enough not to have to stalk men. So if I see him again . . . fine, if not, then it wasn't meant to be."

Trina huffed, but had no choice but to agree. We enjoyed the night, even with her looking over her shoulder and around the room every five minutes for the mystery man. We never ran into him again that night.

"Oh well, I guess it wasn't meant to be," Trina said once the event had ended and we were out in the car about to pull off.

I suddenly let out a chuckle while saying, "I guess it was meant to be."

"Pardon me?"

Had I really said that out loud? I'd forgotten all about the fact that I was even on the phone with Lee.

"Oh, uh, nothing. I'm sorry."

"No need to apologize for blowing me off. You're making it up to me now. So bring your lovely self outside before we're late."

"I'm on my way out." I ended the call and got all giddy and bubbly inside. He'd said to hurry up before we were late. That meant that wherever he was taking me to breakfast we had to have a reservation. "Geesh, I hope I'm dressed right. I should have worn something else," I said, having no idea what an understatement that was when thirty minutes later I found myself sitting inside the sanctuary of Brighton Road Seventh Day Adventist Church in Columbus, Ohio, with my date, Deacon Lee Royce Hampton.

Chapter Two

Eggs Anyone?

The evil thoughts I was thinking during praise and worship were surely to guarantee me a ticket straight to hell, as if that night in Cancun a couple years earlier hadn't already sealed the fate of my eternal destination anyway. But I was thinking of some evil, ugly things right about now. I mean, how could this fine man who looked more like a delicious Dunkin' Donut than a devout deacon trick me into going to church? Now that's what was evil.

I looked up at Lee, who was standing and clapping his hands to some song the choir was singing about the glory of the Lord. He looked down at me, all smiles. I rolled my eyes so hard, I'm surprised they really didn't get stuck like my Ga-Ga used to warn me they would. My obvious attitude had no effect on Lee as he simply kept the smile on his face and turned his attention back to praise and worship.

I let out a harrumph that nobody could hear over that dang on drummer, who by the way was going to work on that drum set. I should be ashamed to admit that the drummer in a church was kind of like the DJ at the club. They seemed to hold the power of whether or not folks were going to get up and get their groove on. Or, in case of church, get their Holy Ghost on. The boom, boom, boom did kind of make me want to get on my feet as well, but that was not about to happen.

My dress was so short that I just knew Sister So-and-so behind me was going to be pointing fingers and whispering to the person on the pew next to her about the way I was dressed.

I looked down at my strapless, too-short sundress. Instead of looking like someone ready to join the Kingdom, I looked like I was pledging for Hoochie-Phi-Hoochie. Oooooh, I was going to get that Lee. He had me up in here looking like a fool. Nobody made Musik Jalice Carter look like a fool except for herself, and that was only after a couple shots of tequila. Since Mr. Deacon Hampton wanted to play games and try to play me, he would get his. Oh, yes, I would spend the rest of my days if need be getting my revenge for this one.

"No weapon formed against me shall prosper . . . Vengeance is mine thus sayeth the Lord." Those were the words to the next song the choir sang. How timely, right?

About one minute into the song my hand subconsciously began to tap my leg. After another two minutes my upper body began to sway. Three minutes in, my eyes would stay closed for a long period of time and my head would uncontrollably nod in agreement with the lyrics. Four minutes in, I found myself standing on my feet next to Lee, and I couldn't care less if the people behind me could see where my skin on the back of my legs starts to darken the closer it got to my buttocks. *I wonder why white people's butts don't get about two to three shades darker than their natural skin complexion like some black people's do. Did my mind really just wander off like that?*

Five minutes into the song, my eyes were watering and I needed the choir to wrap this thing up before I smudged my Mary Kay mascara all over my eyes. *I knew I should have gotten the waterproof kind.* My emotions were just taking over, and all from a song;

a song that was about to have me bawling like a baby. Why wouldn't this song just end already? I know I heard that song one Sunday morning on the radio during the four-hour time slot my favorite station plays gospel music. I'm more than certain that song was not this dang long.

Another minute and I honestly didn't even want the song to ever end. It took me to a place—a foreign land I knew nothing about—but I wasn't scared. All of a sudden I knew the language and the people welcomed me with opened arms. I felt loved. I felt joy, happiness, and peace. It was an indescribable feeling that I didn't want to go away. But then the song faded out and I opened my eyes to discover that my hands were lifted up in the air. I quickly put them down and then looked over to see if Lee had noticed. Heck, for a minute there I had forgotten that Lee was even standing there next to me. I'd forgotten anyone was in the room with me. It felt like it was just me and . . . me and . . . Jesus?

He was standing there with like this light around him or something. No, not Jesus—Lee. His hands were lifted, his head was bowed, and tears were streaming down his face. And he was . . . naked!

Let's just be honest, I was no Mary the Virgin. I'd seen a few naked men in my day. But Lee was the first man I had ever seen naked that was fully dressed. He had stripped himself of everything who he was and only God's light shown on him. It was incredible.

See, God and Jesus was not a tangible thing to me, but Lee was. Right there at that minute I got it. I got the fact that God was using something that was tangible in a nonbeliever's life to show Himself. I saw the God in Lee. Not his hot bod, pretty white teeth, skin that looked like the outer layer of a Reese's Cup that I just wanted to lick and . . . Okay, you get what I'm saying. I didn't see any of those things. All I saw was the God in him. And that was far more attractive than anything else about him.

In spite of how I might have felt a few minutes ago, right now I felt like the luckiest woman in the world. Not only had I just met one man who I could see being in my life forever, but I'd met Lee as well. Jesus and Lee—what more could I ask for?

"Those songs were beautiful. I mean, that choir is . . . is . . . What's the word?" I tried to search for the right words.

"Anointed," Lee said as he sat across the restaurant table from me, taking a bite of his baked chicken.

"Yeah, anointed."

When I went to Mexico I got a book that taught me a little bit of Mexican and Spanish. When I went to Italy I got a book that taught me a little bit of Italian. For Canada, some French. I'd have to visit Amazon.com like ASAP to see if they had a book on how to speak "church."

"That choir was anointed. And that drummer . . . Shelia E. will always be my favorite, but he's a great runner-up. But when ol' girl came out and interpreted every single word of that song with her body and facial expressions, I said look out Destiny's Child. Not one of them four girls got a thing on whatever that stuff ol' girl was doing."

"Liturgical dance," Lee contributed. I think I saw him try to hide a smile that had cracked across his lips. I couldn't tell though because he put his head down and put a bite of mashed potatoes in his mouth.

"Well, whatever it was, it was beautiful. While you were talking to a couple of your church brothers after service, I even went over to her and told her how much I enjoyed her dance. How much she . . . blessed me." Hey, one point for me. I was certain that was church talk. "But that preacher," I continued, shaking my head, and let out an "Umpf, umpf, umpf."

"Yes, Pastor Washington is an awesome man of God," Lee said.

"Could have fooled me. I thought he was God for a minute the way he was talking to me. I swear some of those things he was saying about and to me, I thought only God Himself knew."

"He's no God—just always in God's face. Therefore God knows what to place in the earthly vessel's spirit to deliver to His people." He took a swig of his soda and then added, "God must have known you were going to be there this morning."

"Yeah, He must have." I lifted a forkful of salad to my lips but then halted before placing the greenery in my mouth. I realized that I'd been talking so much—talked on the ride over to the buffet, talked during the buffet line, and now was talking during lunch—that I had forgotten all about giving Lee the business about having me up in church in the first place. "It would have been nice, though, had I known I was going to be there this morning."

Lee's drink must have gone down the wrong pipe because he started choking.

"And I ain't gonna save your slick self either. You sit right there and choke to death. Serves you right for setting me up like that."

Lee cleared his throat and then wiped his mouth. "What?" He shrugged his shoulders and tried his best to hide the smirk that was dying to split his beautiful lips apart. Okay, so we weren't in church anymore. My flesh was still in control and one day in church wasn't going to change that.

"What? What—the fact that we talked on the phone for hours and you didn't mention anything about you being a church boy. You're a dang deacon, Lee. Then you butter me all up for a date, not even mentioning you were taking me to church."

"Ahhh, church was just a pit stop," he downplayed it. "This is the real date." He winked.

"Don't even try it," I scolded playfully, pointing my fork at him and giving him the evil eye. "You know darn well you could have told me how I needed to dress. You let me walk out of the house and flop down into your car wearing next to nothing knowing we were going to the house of the Lord. Do you know how incredibly awkward and embarrassed I felt with all eyes on me?"

Lee stopped and looked at me like I was crazy. "You know darn well folks were not eyeballing you crazy or anything like that."

He was right. Not a single member looked at me sideways. Not one that I noticed anyway. I might as well have been wearing a choir robe for all they cared.

"Girl, you fine and all," Lee said, looking me up and down, "but not finer than Jesus. Trust me, up in my church, Jesus is Lord. All eyes are on Jesus—not on man."

"What about on woman? After all, you took your eyes off Jesus long enough to notice me," I reminded him.

"Yeah, I did. Didn't I?" He took a bite of his chicken, giving me the eye the entire time.

Even though we were making light of the situation, a part of me was still a bit perturbed that Lee had failed to mention anything about him being a deacon or our date being going to his church. I was curious. Maybe concerned was the word. So instead of letting it sit inside, us fall madly in love, get married, start a family, and a part of me wonder if this was all real, making me one angry black woman if it wasn't, I figured I'd better find out now. "Did you use me? Was this whole thing real?"

Lee looked as confused as all get-out. "Is what real?"

"You. Me. Us. Whatever we are going to maybe end up being. Or were you just trying to get a notch on your halo, or earn a halo, or whatever you Christians do when you try to get people to join church, get saved, or whatever?" I shooed my hand, tired of straining my brain on finding the right church words to use so he would understand what I was trying to say.

Lee swallowed hard, like he'd just said the heck with chewing up that chicken. He then dropped his fork to his plate and pushed it away. There was silence as he then picked up his napkin, wiped his mouth, and threw the napkin over his plate. Guess something I'd said had made him lose his appetite.

He took a deep breath, then rested his back against his chair. "Are you asking me did I seek you out just to gain some kind of notoriety in church for evangelizing the lost or something?"

"Don't act like it's farfetched. It could be some tactic you guys use. Go to clubs searching for lost souls to bring to God. Kind of like a . . . a . . ."

"An outreach ministry?"

"Yeah, outreach or something. I mean, what kind of deacon hangs out at Satin Saturday's?"

"A deacon who owns a printing company and had to meet one of his clients there to drop off some marketing and promotional material."

I wanted to excuse myself while I picked my face up off the ground.

"The guys who host Satin Saturday's are one of my clients," Lee started to explain. "I'd just dropped off one of their projects. I was waiting for them to bring me my check. Once they did I left. I wanted to stay and hunt down the beautiful girl who brushed me off while I was waiting, but I had an anniversary party I had to attend. Does that answer your question?"

Ohhh, he told me. I was feeling real embarrassed now. Wearing a little sundress and flip-flops to church was nothing compared to this. "I'm sorry, Lee. But can you blame me? You kept all that a secret. Usually when people keep secrets, it's because they are hiding something or have ulterior motives."

He sighed and leaned in. "I didn't tell you because I didn't want to lose you before I ever even had you."

I was confused by his comment.

"Musik, do you know how many women I've met who I really wanted to get to know better, but before they could even get to really know me at all they cut me off? The minute I mention the fact that I'm a deacon in the church, these women act like I'm the kryptonite to their every fantasy. There are a few women who couldn't care less. They are the ones who were too busy trying to convert me in order for me to convert them, if you know what I mean."

I knew exactly what he meant with that convicting comment of his. I, myself, had only been a thought away from trying to convert him over to my team of fornicating sinners. *Dang it!*

"But you're different, Musik."

Huh, if only he knew.

"You just have this air about you that is vivid and clear. You don't blow smoke. So for some crazy reason, with you I was compelled to keep that bit of information about me being a deacon and all on the back burner. Don't get me wrong, in no way shape or form am I denying Christ. I just felt this was the right way to go about it. I wanted to show you instead of tell you." He rested his case, looking at me as if he was expecting my closing arguments. Then the verdict.

I thought for a moment, leaned in, and simply said, "Well, I'm kind of glad you decided to show me rather than tell me. I'm a strong believer that actions speak louder than words. And, well, Mr. Hampton, or should I say Deacon Hampton, I liked what I saw."

He leaned in as well. "And, well, Ms. Carter, I love what I see."

I wanted to melt in his hands. He smiled one of his bright smiles and then I changed my mind. I wanted to melt in his mouth instead, repenting a few seconds later for that thought. This was going to be hard, kicking it with a Christian dude. A fine, sexy Christian dude at that. Why did God have to go and make Christian men so sexy? Just seems like an oxymoron to me. I'd have to put my guard up. He could see me as the hellion I was—non-convertible—and decide to drop me because our egg yolks didn't mix up, scramble, or something like that.

"So, what do you say, Ms. Carter? Willing to get to know me better and see what God has in store? I'm not asking you to give up the life you live. Do your thing, ma. Be the woman you are. But if I do my job right as a man—a man of God—then, eventually, you'll end up being a reflection of me regardless. So do you think you can hang with an old church boy like myself? Do you?" He waited all cool, calm, and collected like he was at a detail shop waiting for his Jaguar to get finished up.

"I do, Mr. Hampton. I do," I confessed. I had no idea how this thing with Lee and me was going to work, with him being into church and me not. But who cared about all that business about yolks and stuff? I had to take my chances with this man. Besides, I wasn't a big fan of eggs anyway.

Chapter Three

Did He Really?

"I do, I do, and I do. And just in case you didn't hear me, I do again!"

The minister and the two witnesses at the Vegas chapel couldn't hold in their laughter. Neither could Lee as I professed to take him as my lawfully wedded husband.

Vegas wasn't necessarily the wedding I envisioned in my fairytale, but who cared? I was marrying the man I had dated for the last nine years. Come to think of it, the proposal wasn't necessarily the proposal I envisioned in my fairytale either. There was no knight in shining armor down on one knee professing his undying and everlasting love for me. There was no ring. As a matter of fact, there really wasn't even a proposal.

Through all nine years of our relationship and all the drama, Lee and I had managed to have two children and no wedding. When I say drama, it wasn't anything serious. There were just a few disagreements here and there. Then there was a season of nothing but arguments. In all honesty, I was the argumentative one. Lee hated fussing and fighting, but I couldn't help it. I was just so bitter and hurt. My underlying emotions were a result of me just harboring issues with Lee, because in my mind, he was the root of my bitterness and hurt.

Ironically, the best thing that ever happened to me in life, falling in love with Lee, was like a double-edged sword. It was the thing that was drumming up all the tension I was having with Lee. After almost a decade, he'd made me the mother of his children, but he had not made me his wife. I had a major problem with that, but I didn't want to speak on it because I didn't want him to think I was pressuring him. I didn't want to have to tell a man that I wanted him to make me his wife. I wanted a man to tell me that he wanted to make me his wife. But Lee just seemed so content living together and having babies. That truly surprised me, considering how into church he was. But that all had changed too.

There was a period of six months when Lee's job transferred him to a neighboring city. The kids and I stayed at the house we'd bought in Columbus and his job got him a little one-bedroom apartment. His church duties and obligations had already started taking a back seat to his job, but this move ushered church completely out of life. His life, not mine. Me and the kids were attending church every single Sunday. Our presence in the house of the Lord went without saying. Eventually I even joined the dance ministry. That's when things got real for me.

About three months into my being on the dance ministry, the pastor felt led to have the dance leader draw up a mission statement, vision, and bylaws. Part of the dance ministry mission statement was that we present our bodies to Christ holy and acceptable. Immediate conviction swept through my spirit. How could I lie down with Lee, a man who wasn't my husband, then get on that altar every Sunday and minister with that same body? I even asked God to give me exceptions.

"Lord, Lee and I have been together over eight years. That's longer than some marriages last. And we have kids together. We're practically one. We're practically married."

God agreed that He would give me a pass if I could show Him in His word, the Bible, where He stated that such exceptions could be made to that particular commandment of "Thou shall not fornicate."

I couldn't. I knew right then that even though God had an anointing on the ministry of dance He'd placed in me, I would not be able to go to the levels and dimensions He'd called me to if my life did not line up with His Word. Needless to say I sat Lee down and told him that from that point on he could no longer put his hand in the cookie jar. The bakery was closed. No more getting the cookie until after we got a wedding cake. Period. Point blank.

Everybody thought I was crazy for doing that. Believe it or not, even some church folks thought I was wrong for doing that to Lee. I stuck to my guns though. I feared the Lord more than I feared Lee's reaction to my commitment to the Lord. Needless to say, Lee did not take it well.

He was livid at my decision not to break him off even a chocolate chip. He being the one who introduced me to the Father, the Son, and Holy Ghost, I was just sure he would support my decision. Not!

By then, Lee and I had completely flipped roles when it came to church. He didn't even go on the Sundays he was in town, complaining he was too tired from the drive in after work the night before.

My commitment wasn't to the church, though. It was to God. And I'm so proud to say that even on nights when Lee would put me out the bed because he couldn't stand being next to me not being able to touch me, I stayed true. I didn't give up. I didn't give in. For nine months I didn't even turn the oven on to bake cookies.

There was more tension than ever in our relationship to say the least. That was one of the reasons why we decided to take a family trip to Vegas. We wanted to have fun and get things back on track.

"We should just get married while we're in Vegas." That suggestion was made about a month before we were set to leave on the trip. I honestly can't even remember who said it. The other agreed. And now there we stood in a Vegas chapel exchanging vows. No big wedding. And with Lee being the oldest child and the first to marry, his mother was not too thrilled about being deprived of having a great big wedding with all the bells and whistles for her child.

She blamed me. She never said it straight out like that. But I could tell. Little did she know it was Lee who didn't want to have a big wedding. He didn't want to make a big to-do. It was right then and there when I should have questioned whether he even wanted to be married at all. He'd said "I do," but did he really?

For the next six years I tormented myself with that question. Had Lee really been so deeply in love with me that he wanted to spend the rest of his life with me? It was hard for me to give a wholehearted yes. After all, he hadn't planned a decent proposal. Heck, even an indecent proposal would have been sufficient. He didn't want a big wedding or any of his family to even fly out to Vegas and witness the exchange of our vows. He never went out and bought me a wedding band. I'd picked one up for each of us at a Walmart just for the sake of having something to exchange during the ceremony. He didn't even rent a tux. Not even a suit jacket. He married me in a cotton shirt. He would go out and buy suits for his company's management meetings, but he bought a cotton shirt for our exchange of vows— something he should have deemed far more special. In my heart it was special.

Lee didn't make it seem special in any way. It was like he was saying to me without actually speaking the words, "What the heck? I been with this chick nine years. I've already spent the best years of my prime with her, we got two kids, I done bought a house. I got too much invested in this. And on top of it all, who wants to come to Vegas and not get any cookie? Might as well get married and just get it over with."

Even when Lee would introduce me as his wife, it just seemed so mechanical. There was no pride behind the introduction. No feeling. I wanted to feel something. I wanted him to feel like D'Angelo did in that song, "You're My Lady." I wanted him to make me feel like that woman in that song. I needed him to make me feel that way. What woman didn't want her man to make her believe that she was the only woman in the world? That she was the only woman he had eyes for? That she was the only woman he could ever see himself lying down with? Even if it wasn't a realistic truth, a woman still wanted that from her man. She needed that from her man.

At the end of the day, I can't believe Lee and I ended up being unequally yoked after all. How so? Well, the answer to that is simple: I was in love with Lee—deeply in love with Lee. Lee only loved me. This is why our now six years of marriage hasn't been that electric. I started holding myself back from Lee. I was too scared to give him all of me knowing that I was barely getting half of him. It was miserable, but we had kids. I'd wanted this marriage more than anything. I couldn't bail out now. I'd had fifteen years to see our relationship for what it was. I guess maybe those bright smiling teeth of his really had blinded me. I couldn't see that I was pushing for and wanting things that Lee might not have wanted.

I was happier than Shug Avery in *The Color Purple* when she finally stopped giving away the cookie without a ring and got married. I, too, was shouting out from the rooftop, "I's married now." I loved the status of being married, but I had great doubts of whether Lee did. Then one day my doubts were completely erased. I knew for sure he didn't grab hold of and wear the status of marriage as proudly as I did. If he had, then the day I finally went to his www.FaceIt.com social networking page I would have seen his relationship status as married. But I didn't. His relationship status was blank. Now why wouldn't he want to shout it from the rooftop as well that he was married? I had no idea, but I became hell-bent on finding out!

Chapter Four

Friend Request

Let's rewind it about a week or so prior to me discovering Lee's relationship status on FaceIt. I'd spent an entire day setting up my FaceIt page. It was so fun plugging in all that information the profile page asked for. My family was my life so I spent a great deal of time posting wedding pics, pictures of the kids playing sports and whatnot. I started getting friend requests immediately. I began searching for people who I knew and sent them friend requests. When I searched for Lee's name and he popped up, of course I sent him a friend request.

After a while I gave FaceIt a rest for the evening, but was excited to get back on it the next day and begin networking.

I was new to social networking. Lee and some of my other friends had been on FaceIt for years. My pastor had always voiced his disdain for the public networking site, so I never had a desire to engage in it. But the more I started going to work-related conferences and realized that half the folks already knew each other and had relationships with one another because of that Web site, I knew I had to get with the times. And so I did.

I accepted most of the friend requests and even had a couple of FaceIt inbox messages. All of the friend requests I had sent had been accepted. All except for one: Lee's.

"His should have been the first to accept," I told myself. *Maybe he just hasn't been on FI to see that I sent him a request.* But a couple more days went by and still no acceptance. Then a couple more went by. There was still no acceptance.

"Hmmm, let me try to send him another one. Maybe I thought I sent him one and really didn't." When I attempted to send Lee a friend request I got a prompt stating that I'd already sent one. That's when I decided to do something I hadn't done yet: go check out Lee's FI page and see if he'd been on it. But I was almost certain he had. Every time I put the kids to bed and came into our bedroom he was on the computer. I'd imagined he'd checked in on his FI page while on the computer.

Once I searched for Lee's page and it came up, I was taken directly to his information page. I was excited to see all the information he had listed.

My breath got caught in my throat when I saw that he hadn't mentioned anywhere the fact that he was married and had a family. I was so hurt. He was my world. I thought I was his. I know FaceIt didn't define our relationship, but it did let me know where his head was at when it came to what he thought about me.

If you ask me, a person's family and most important things in life should be one of the first things they would want to share and talk about with the world. The fact that Lee had a beautiful wife and family at home shouldn't have dominated the page, but it should have at least been prevalent somewhere. I didn't give a crap about his favorite book, movie, or interests. I cared about his favorite girl—me.

The more I scrolled his FaceIt page, the more I realized that I was nonexistent. How was it that he had pictures of his mother, siblings, aunts, uncles, nieces, nephews, but none of his wife? Heck, he even had a picture of his prized Corvette. And here all this time I thought I was his prize. And should I even humiliate myself a step further to mention that he even took a picture of the jersey of his favorite sports team and put it on FI?

I had no idea tears had began falling from my eyes until I began questioning where all the drops of water that were hitting my keyboard were coming from. Yes, I'd questioned my role in Lee's life, if I was as big a part of his life as he was of mine. It was devastating to find that, let his FaceIt page tell it, I wasn't a part of his life at all. I wasn't even a second thought. I wasn't a thought at all. Had I even been a mere thought I would have been somewhere, anywhere on his FaceIt page.

As I searched his FI page for even a remnant of the fact that Lee was a married man, I realized that my access was limited. I had to be a friend of his to get the full scope of his page: things he posted, pages he liked, people he was subscribed to, and people he was friends with. But I wasn't his friend. Heck, let him tell it, I wasn't even his wife.

I was fired up. Everything in me wanted to call Lee up on the phone and confront him with my findings, but I knew if I did that, he would never accept my friend request. I needed to be his friend to actually find out if there was anything I should be worried about—anything like him not just hiding me, but him hiding someone from me, like a woman. From women. Despite popular opinion, it wasn't just men who got on social networking sites to seek out women. There were women who were convinced God had told them their husband was on FI. And as long as they thought Lee was available, what was keeping them from trying to make my husband theirs?

"Oh, heck to the naw!" I said out loud, grabbing my cell phone and calling Lee up.

"Hey, wife, I was just about to call you," was Lee's greeting.

Hearing his voice calmed the raging lion inside of me. "Oh really? For what?" My voice was snappy, so maybe his voice hadn't completely calmed me.

"Just to see how your day is going. I know you work from home and all, but still, I know you have all your clients and projects and deadlines and stuff. I'm just making sure everything's good with you. What time is Lee Jr.'s soccer game this evening?"

He sounded like such the family man. But on paper, the computer, FI, he was anything but the family man. So was this all an act he was giving me? Had our entire relationship been an act? Did marrying me just make sense? Was I just this woman he could live with, but not the woman he couldn't live without?

"Musik, you still there?"

Lee's inquiry jarred me out of my thoughts. "Hey, huh, what? Yeah, I'm here."

"Well, what are you up to?"

"Nothing . . ." That was all I was going to say, but then decided to open the door to discuss what was really on my mind. "Just setting up this FI page. I finally decided to join the modern world and get into this social networking stuff." I chuckled.

He matched my chuckle with a chuckle, only his sounded nervous.

"By the way, didn't you get my friend request?" Patience never was a virtue of mine.

He paused way too long before he decided to say, "Yeah, I did." I could tell he'd used the pause to debate whether to tell me the truth. That was a red flag for me.

"Oh, then why didn't you accept the request?" I was so proud of myself for not sounding combative.

"I just haven't gone into my friend requests and accepted them yet. I'll do it when I get home."

Liar! Liar! Liar! He was lying. He knew darn well that, had I not mentioned that friend request, there was no way he would have accepted it. Nothing burned me more than someone lying to me. There was another reason why people lied: because they didn't want the person to know the truth. Lies hide the truth.

What do you have to hide from me, Lee Hampton? What do you have to hide?

When Lee got home that evening he did his normal routine. He got on the treadmill, took a shower, ate dinner, and then . . . and then that's when his routine changed. He climbed in bed and turned on the television. Yes, that last thing was part of his schedule, but something was missing. It was that something that came in between eating and watching TV in bed. Tonight, for some odd reason, Lee didn't hop on his computer.

Men are creatures of habit. The minute they change their routine is the minute yet another red flag shall rise.

"You tired?" I said, entering our bedroom after putting the kids to bed, to see Lee flipping through channels. I was very much surprised that he wasn't on his computer.

"Uh, no, I'm good," he said, his eyes glued to CNN.

"Good." With my laptop in hand, I sat down next to him and powered it up. "Go ahead and accept my friend request so I can start building my number of friends."

"Oh, wife, do I have to do it right now? I'm chillin'."

"It's just the click of a mouse. You're good." After all, he'd just said he was good.

I went to the FI homepage and then slid the laptop over to Lee. He sighed before sitting up and logging into his account. He acted like my asking him to accept my FI friend request was like asking him to move a mountain.

"Here you go. We're friends now," he said, and, if I'm not mistaken, there was a hint of sarcasm in his tone.

"Thanks, *friend*." I smiled and then logged into my own FI account. Of course, once I was logged in I went straight to surfin' Lee's page. I could see everything now. Still, there was not even the slightest sign that he was married with kids. I scrolled through some of his past posts. He mentioned how he was going to visit his family, how he had gone somewhere with his mom, how he had had fun with his cousin, friend, or whoever, but not even a "Hey, my wife and I just enjoyed this great movie." Not even a "My wife and I had a great time here or there." Nothing.

I scrolled back as far as I could, looking for a post where he had mentioned me and his family just once— us on a family vacation or something. Still there was nothing. I felt like nothing. He made me feel like nothing. I felt erased.

"Aren't you coming to bed, wife?"

I wanted him to stop calling me that. If he couldn't fix his black, ashy fingers to type it, then he shouldn't have fixed his lips to say it. No, his fingers aren't really all that black and certainly not ashy, but dang it, I was mad!

I looked down at the clock on the computer. Two hours had easily passed. I couldn't believe I'd spent all that time stalking his FI page. I'd found nothing—but not a good nothing, if you know what I mean. I realized that I was wasting my time; I wasn't going to find myself in him.

I logged off and slammed the laptop closed. "Yeah, I'm coming to bed." With that being said, I set the computer on the nightstand next to me, pulled the cover up to my neck, and bade him a "Good night."

I could feel his confused eyes staring at my back as I lay there pondering whether I should say anything. He chose to let me be and instead got on his own laptop and logged on to the computer. I'm not sure how long I lay there hurt, fuming, and confused. I kept asking myself, was I being rational about all this? Was what my spouse put on FI really that serious? Was it enough to have me feeling like I had no place in his life after all these years? I asked both myself and God those questions. I didn't have any answers. I'm sure God did, but He didn't tell me that night; not before I fell off to sleep anyway.

The next morning everything was routine. Lee headed out to work and I got the kids off to school. After my morning prayer session I logged on to my computer to see if I had any e-mails from my clients. What I discovered was that my FI page was connected to my e-mail account. There were e-mails of FI notifications in my inbox. That, of course, prompted me to start thinking about the whole FI/Lee situation all over again, which led me to sign on FI and go peruse his FI page again.

I thought I was going to have a heart attack when I clicked on to his page and discovered that things I had just been able to view last night I could no longer view.

What stood out the most was that his friends list was now on "privacy." I was no longer privy to see exactly who all of his FI friends were.

"What the . . . But why?" *Lee must have changed all his settings last night*. There was no way this was a coincidence. There was no way he just happened to decide to change all his privacy settings the very same day he accepted my friend request. That was some BS if I ever smelled it, stepped it in, and whatever else.

This did more than just set off a red flag. The bull was in the ring ready to destroy and rip that stupid red flag to shreds. And if you haven't figured it out by now, I was the bull—in a china shop. And before I tore up the whole place, I needed to confront Lee. I needed answers. *And they better had be the right answers; otherwise, not only will the china shop be destroyed beyond repair, so will our marriage.*

Chapter Five

Just Face It—It's Over!

"So why all of a sudden do you have the privacy set on your FI page?" I blared into the phone at Lee. No, I couldn't wait for him to get home from work to discuss this matter. I wouldn't be able to think straight the rest of the day until I got to the bottom of things.

"Girl, what are you talking about?" He let out one of those stupid nervous chuckles again.

"You know exactly what I'm talking about, that's why you doing that stupid little laugh you do," I quipped. "Just last night I was able to see who your friends on FI were, now all of a sudden it's blocked out. Who you blockin' it from, Lee? Huh? Me? Of course you are. Who are you trying to hide from me, Lee? I mean it's obvious you're hiding me from everybody else, but who exactly are you trying to hide from me?" I was on fire to say the least. Five alarm up in this piece!

"Wife, you are trippin'." Lee tsked.

"Wife? Oh now I'm your wife, but let your FI page tell it, you ain't even married. Why is it that you answered every other stupid question for your profile page—your favorite book, movie, sports, interest, hobbies, home-town, blah blah blah—but you skipped the question about your relationship status? Seriously, Lee, how did you think that was gonna make me feel?" That time I actually paused to give him time to answer the question.

"It's my FI page so, to be honest with you, I wasn't thinking about how it would make you feel. My FI page isn't about you. It's about me. That's why it's *my* FI page. You do what you want with yours and I'll do what I want with mine. You been on FaceIt a hot minute and I've been on it almost two years and already you trying to regulate what I do on it. My FI page is my own personal sanctuary."

"Boo, your prayer closet is your own personal sanctuary. FI is a public social network. The keyword is 'public.' That means everybody and they mama have the ability to know what's going on with you and in your life. And it's obvious that the life you live does not include me."

"What do you mean it does not include you? Woman, I come home to you every night. I go to work every day so that I can provide for you and the kids. I don't go hanging out with my friends and come home at all hours of the night. I'm your husband, and as your husband you ain't never had no other woman calling you up talking trash about her being with your husband. You ain't never had to call up no other women. I pay the bills, handle my business, so why are you tripping about what I did or didn't put on a social networking page?"

"I care because I'm your wife. I'm your woman. Like D'Angelo said in his song, I'm your lady. I want you to be proud of that fact, proud enough where that's the first thing you want to share with people. I want you to show me that I'm a big part of your life, but I can see clearly that I'm not a part of your life at all—not a part you care to tell people about. Why is that, Lee? Why is it you have a picture of every member of your family except for your wife and kids? Negro, you even took the time to take a picture of your car and put it on FI. Really?"

"What did I tell you about calling me the 'N' word?"

"Is that all you heard me say? Out of everything I just said to you, spilling my guts about how I feel, all you heard was the word 'Negro.' Wow!"

"Wow is right," Lee countered. "I'm at work and you are calling me up about some FI stuff. I'm not about to have you mess my entire day up over this mess. Not doing it right now, Musik. When I get home, we'll talk. Cool?"

"Funny how you have managed to not answer a single one of my questions." I shook my head. "Sure, Lee, we can talk when you get home. That will give your sorry behind the entire day to get your lies together. Deuces . . . Negro." I slammed down the phone, even angrier than I was before I picked up the phone.

I couldn't believe how nonchalant he was acting about this entire thing. That's when I had to ask myself whether Lee was being nonchalant or I was being overdramatic. I wanted to pick up the phone and call friends of mine who were married and ask them how they would feel if they were in my shoes. Would they be bothered by the fact that their husband failed to answer the question regarding his relationship status on his social networking profile page? Would they be bothered by the fact that he had pics posted of everybody he knew except for his wife? Would they be hurt by this?

Who gives a crap if another woman would or would not be hurt? I'm hurt. I'm hurting. For all these years I hoped that deep inside I meant just as much to Lee as he meant to me. I hoped that for all these years he was just as happy to claim me as his wife as I was to claim him as my husband. For all these years . . .

My thoughts trailed off because now I was lying to myself. Complete and utter lies were exactly what I was telling myself. When Lee and I first hooked up, it wasn't love at first sight. I didn't look at him and say, "That's going to be the man I marry." Neither did he look at me and say, "That is going to be the woman I marry." We were both dating around, but for me, the moment did come when I knew he was the one. The moment did come when I picked up the phone and cut off every other guy I had been dating. I'd found what I was looking for and I knew it.

When it comes to Lee, he did the same thing with the women he'd been dating, but it wasn't for the same reasons as mine.

I'd started spending the night at his place and hanging out there so much that I had to give my peoples his phone number in order to reach me. I didn't have a cell phone yet back then. Knowing that sometimes when his phone rang it would be for me, I started answering it. Now that I think back, I realize Lee never gave me permission to answer his phone. I just assumed he'd be okay with it. I'd just assumed he'd already cut off the other women. I'd just assumed he'd chosen me over them. Had I assumed way too much? Had Lee really wanted me as his girl or had I just staked a claim and marked my territory? I chose him, but had he ever really chosen me?

"Nooo!" I yelled out, feeling like Carrie narrating a scene about her and Mr. Big from *Sex and the City*. What had I done? Had I forced Lee into a relationship with me? I became sick to my stomach at every thought that confirmed that could be the case. My thoughts eventually led up to our wedding. Had I done the ultimate no-no and forced Lee into a marriage?

I'd wanted the marriage so bad. He'd wanted the sex so bad. I declared a vow of celibacy nine years into our relationship. He couldn't take not having sex after nine months. We got married.

"Jesus!" I was still crying out. Had my entire act of celibacy really been about God, or had it been about getting Lee to marry me?

If my life was a lie, I was the one who had orchestrated it. But how would I ever truly know if Lee's feelings for me had been natural and genuine or dictated by me?

Tears streamed down my face as I tried to think back, look back for a sign, any sign, that what Lee and I had all of these years was real, but I couldn't find not a one. Technically, he never officially asked me to be his girl. Technically, he never officially asked me to be his wife. But, worst of all, technically, he never officially asked me to be a part of his life.

I remained in a complete daze for the rest of the day, not getting a lick of work done. It was a surreal feeling. My entire relationship had been one-sided. I'd been madly in love with Lee, but that hadn't been the case with him. Or maybe it had been. How would I ever truly know? Asking him wouldn't suffice. He'd just tell me what I wanted to hear, or maybe it would be the truth. But actions speak louder than words anyway. Lining up Lee's actions over the years, and now his actions with this whole FI thing, I had my answers. Had I given Lee the option and free will, there is a highly likely chance that he and I would have never gotten into an exclusive relationship in the first place. Let alone be married.

The life I was living wasn't necessarily the one Lee was supposed to be living. I felt so stupid, and at first I felt guilty until I spurt out, "Why didn't he just tell me then? Why didn't he just man up and have the testicles to just say it instead of going along as if this was what he wanted?"

There, I'd managed to turn the tables and get fired up at Lee again. It wasn't like I was trying to shift blame. I'd been 100 percent real with Lee throughout our entire relationship. My feelings, what I wanted, they'd all been genuine. But my gut, my woman's intuition, told me that Lee had not been. And it took a simple FI profile to bring the situation to light.

Speaking of FI, I decided to get on it. If Lee wanted to eliminate me from his life, I'd eliminate him from mine. I'd let him see how it felt not to be included in my virtual world.

I grabbed the first laptop at my fingertips, which happened to be Lee's, and opened it up to log on to my account so that I could defriend him. Lo and behold, it was already logged on to FI.

"Lee must have forgotten to sign off last night," I said to myself. Just as my finger was about to exit out of his account and sign into mine, a light bulb went off in my head. I was in his account. I was actually inside Lee's FI account. Whatever it was he had been trying to hide from me . . . hot dog, I was about to find it.

The first thing I did was check out his friends list. It was eighty percent women who were not related to him, five percent men who were not related to him, and the other fifteen percent was family.

Now I remembered once upon a time Lee telling me that he was getting on FI to reconnect and keep up with old friends. *You mean to tell me all his friends are women? Can't be.* I'd been in his life fifteen years and surely I would have known or even heard of some of these so-called friends. What really ticked me off was when I did a second run through of the list and recognized some of the names. A couple were the names of women he'd dated before. Now why in the world would a married man want to reconnect and keep up with an ex? Why would any married person want to do that? They were an ex for a reason and it should stay that way. The past doesn't mix with the present and can sure enough mess up the future if you hang on to it long enough.

Next, I went through his photo album to look at who "liked" the photos Lee had posted or who had made comments. I ended up having to grab a pen and paper to keep a tally. There were about ten women who always seemed to comment or like every little thing Lee posted. They were virtual groupies. Yuck!

I took that list and began visiting each of their pages to find out a little bit about them. It appeared as though Lee was showing them the same kind of love they'd shown him. Every time they took a picture of themselves in the bathroom and posted it, Lee was there to "like" and comment on it. The only picture he should have been liking of a woman posing was his wife—me.

Next I went to see the type of people and things Lee was subscribing to. Again, my heart did flips when I saw that he was subscribed to strippers or women who did nothing but post provocative pictures of themselves or post sexually charged comments.

"Why?" I asked myself as tears streamed down my face. What was wrong with me? Wasn't I enough to look at? To me, this was just as bad as finding a hidden collection of dirty magazines. Why wasn't just looking at me enough to do it for him? At that moment my self-esteem went from ten to two.

I clicked on each and every photo of those women, trying to figure out what it was about them that Lee liked looking at so much. "They're not me. That's what he likes," I concluded. I was nothing like those women. Built nothing like them. Shaped nothing like them. So if that's what Lee liked, then he didn't like me.

The tears came even harder. I thought I was everything he wanted in a woman. I was forty, but I didn't look it. I was still in pretty good shape. Yeah, I had a baby pouch from giving birth to two kids, but I was still able to fit comfortably in a size ten and suck in my stomach so that it wasn't all flabby and hanging. Still, I guess all that wasn't enough.

Next I decided to visit Lee's message page and check out some of his inbox conversations.

Send me some naked pictures of you?

I had to read that single sentence again.

Send me some naked pictures of you?

Lee had sent some woman that message.

Don't have any, was her reply.

Dang her reply. I was more concerned about my husband's inquiry to her.

The fact that he felt he could ask her that question meant that he was comfortable with her. But just how comfortable were he and this woman?

I looked through some of their past correspondence and saw a message from him asking her: What are you doing?

She replied: Cleaning my house.

Sometime later in that same day he hit her up with that initial question again and she replied: Still cleaning up.

Then he replied: But your place isn't that big. Why is it taking you so long? Did you move or something?

That was it for me. Before I knew it I was crying tears of not only hurt and pain, but rage. "How do you know how big her house is, Lee?" I was screaming at the computer screen as if it would answer. "'Cause you've obviously been in her house. That's how."

I was in physical pain at this point. Picturing my husband with this woman tore me up inside. Trying to digest the fact that my husband would even be corresponding with another woman like this broke me down. It broke me down to nothing. I couldn't take it anymore. I couldn't handle it. I'd seen enough.

I went to close the computer, but being the typical woman, I wanted to know more about the woman who had lured my husband away from being 100 percent faithful to me. I clicked on her profile page and rummaged through her photos. That's when I spotted her and a picture of Lee. His arm was around her. His arm being around her wasn't what caught my eye because there were other people standing around them. Lots of people were hugging. It was a group photo. A work group photo. This woman worked with him.

This was too much for me to bear. I could no longer breathe. My imagination was running wild all over the place. Had I caught Lee in the actual act of cheating? As far as I was concerned I had. Whether it's emotional or physical, to me it's cheating. My husband belonged to me. All of him. His body and his mind. The moment he decided to share another part of himself with another woman was the moment he became a cheater.

When had my husband become a cheater? I had no idea. Was it pre- or post-FI? Had what started out to be nice friendly communications with persons of the opposite sex turned into something more? How much more? And who had initiated it, Lee or the other women? I had no idea. All I knew is that it was over. We were over. What Lee and I had was over. The sad part of it all was that more than likely it had never begun. It had all been just a fairytale, something made up in my mind. And now I had awakened from a fifteen-year dream into a nightmare.

Chapter Six

On and Poppin'

"Kammi, please just hurry up over here and pick up these kids. I'll give you money to take them out to eat, to get ice cream, McDonald's or something. Just please come pick up your niece and nephew, because when their daddy gets home, it's on and poppin'." I was in complete ghetto mode as I spoke to my sister. I was bouncing around on the couch while I talked like Tamar Braxton. One more minute and I was about to start talking in third person and adding the words "dot com" to the end of everything. My marriage was about to be over and I was going out with a bang. I just didn't want my kids to be around. Trust me, the loud explosion would have damaged their poor little eardrums for life.

"Musik, will you calm your happy tail down and tell me what's going on?" Kammi urged.

"I really can't right now." I couldn't right now and I wouldn't later. I'd made it a point in the entire fifteen years of my relationship with Lee to never, and I mean never, share our relationship and marital issues with other people. And even though in my mind just as sure as the sky was blue I was about to end our relationship, I still had no intention of telling anyone exactly what was going on. For one, it was embarrassing. I didn't want anyone to know my husband was just like the

next man. I'd placed him on a pedestal. He walked on
water as far as I was concerned. And now to have to admit that he was on the same level as the next man who
didn't know how to love, respect, and take care of his
woman emotionally—nope, I couldn't do it.

For two, I didn't want to put a certain perception of
Lee in people's heads. Sometimes when a woman is mad
at her man because he's done something hurtful, she
can tend to make things sound worse than they are. A
woman can also provoke someone else (like her sista,
girlfriends, mama, et cetera . . .) to feel just as angry with
her man as she is. Then if and when she patches things
back up with her man, the others she ran her mouth
to about him hold a grudge. They will even look at the
woman like she's crazy for still being involved with ol'
dude. Then she has her girlfriends and her mama still
hating her man for hurting her, et cetera . . . It's just too
messy. It can have a chick choosing between who to kick
it with: her man or her girls.

The main reason, though, after all these years that
I'd never been one to tell my business with Lee was
because I knew the minute I let someone else into our
business, the minute it was no longer just our business.
I don't care if it's good or it's bad, I had always considered my relationship with Lee just that—ours. Our relationship did not need to be the topic of anybody else's
conversation. Period.

"I'm sorry, Kammi, you know me," I told her. "I
ain't the type who needs a shoulder to cry on. I handle
mine—just me and God. Now can you swoop by and
pick up your niece and nephew or what?"

She sighed. "Girl, yeah. I'm already out and about
anyway, about five minutes from your house. Have
them ready."

"Thanks, sis. I appreciate it."

I ended the call and got the kids ready to go with their Auntie Kammi. Once she had picked them up, I started watching the clock. It was 6:00 P.M. Lee had sent me a text stating that he was going to the gym before coming home. I knew he was just stalling. He knew what he had to deal with once he brought his butt home.

The waiting was killing me. I decided to get back on FI. This time I logged into my own account and just went to peruse Lee's page. After typing his name into the search box it didn't pop up. After several tries I decided to scroll down my friends list. Lo and behold, Lee's name was no longer there. I scratched my head, trying to figure out just what the heck was going on.

One of Lee's sisters had accepted my friend request, so I went to her page and searched Lee's name. Perhaps I could click on it from there. Strangely enough, Lee's name showed up nowhere on her page either. Had this fool taken down his FI page trying to destroy the evidence?

I immediately raced over to his laptop, where I had not logged out of his FI account at all. The account was still there on the screen just as bright as day. So why was it that I couldn't get to it? I played around with his page a little bit until I noticed an option that would allow me to manage "blocked persons."

"That Negro better not have," I said as I clicked buttons on the keyboard. "I swear on everything he better not have . . ."

He had. Lee had blocked me from his FI page. At the realization, all I could do was bury my face into my hands. Nobody on earth could tell me that, unless Lee had something to hide, he would not have: one, defriended me; and two, blocked me from being able to view his page altogether.

First I wasn't even a part of his life as far as FI was concerned. Now I wasn't even allowed into his FI life. But we were married. We were a couple. We were one. I know in a relationship each partner deserves a level of privacy, but I repeat—this is a social network. There is no such thing as privacy. I could not grasp how it was okay for strangers to be privy to Lee's life in that aspect but not his wife. I was supposed to be closer to him than anybody. If he couldn't be himself—be who he wanted to be—around me, then he shouldn't have felt comfortable being that way around anybody else either.

Was that what it was? With me now on FI did Lee feel that he couldn't be himself? Post what he wanted to post? Say what he wanted to say? I didn't want a man who couldn't be himself around me. I needed a man who was the same around me, his mama, kids, cat, dog, whoever. I never wanted to feel like I was with a stranger—like, who was this person? Which side of this person did I marry? But that's exactly how I was feeling, and as I heard the garage door opening, a sign that Lee was about to pull in, I was about to find out just who Lee was, how many sides to him there were. And I promise you, I was about to let each and every side of him have it.

More importantly, I was about to find out that out of all those different sides of him that existed, which one I had married. Then I would ask that side for a divorce.

Chapter Seven

You Did It to Yourself

"You blocked me from your FI page? Really, Lee? Your wife?" He'd only had one foot in the door before I started in.

"Look, I said we could talk about this and that's what we are going to do, so just calm down." He set his gym bag down and walked by me, heading up the steps to our bedroom.

Oooohhhh, I wanted to clobber him on the back of his big head. He should have entered the house on his knees begging for forgiveness, yet he was letting it be known with his demeanor that he was running things.

"Then get to talking," I spat, entering the bedroom right behind him.

He exhaled and flopped down on a little bench we had at the foot of our bed. "I blocked you because you can't handle it. You can't handle us being FI friends. You are going to be looking into and analyzing every little thing I do on FI and I'm not trying to deal with that." He began mocking me, using his fingers to make quotation marks in the air. "'Why are you friends with so and so? Why did you "like" her profile pic?' I'm not trying to deal with this every day."

"Well, just so you know, it doesn't matter that you blocked me from FI. You forgot to sign off of your account last night, dummy. I've been in your account and looking at your pages, posts, inbox messages, and everything all day."

All I'm saying is that I wish I'd had a camera to snap the look on his face and update it to be his profile pic. He looked like he'd swallowed the canary—feathers hanging all out his mouth. Everything was dead silent as if the world had stopped spinning.

"Yeah, so you know that life you livin', the one without me? I know all about it now." My anger turned to hurt. How could he have had a life without me? How could he not want me to be a part of everything in his world? Virtual or reality? "Strippers, Lee? You subscribe to strippers? Why? Are you a pervert or something? Did you think for one minute how it would make your wife feel to see that you are subscribed to something like that? Did you think about me at all?

"Did you think about how your wife would feel not to see a single picture of herself on your FI page? Two years is plenty of time for you to have thought about me just once and posted a pic of me—us. How do you think it made me feel not to see you mention my name or that you even have a wife? When someone else has a birthday, you made a solid effort to give them a birthday shout out on your page. Never once did you give a birthday shout out to your wife. No 'today is my anniversary'—nothing."

I had not wanted to break down crying in front of him. I mean, a part of me kept saying, *Girl, listen to yourself; all this over a social networking site. Fifteen years ruined over FI?*

But then there was that other part of me that just felt erased—nonexistent.

In less than a week my value as a wife had depreciated just as much as the houses in our subdivision.

"Musik, just let me explain," Lee started.

"What in the world is there to explain? My eyes don't need an explanation for what they read and what they saw. My heart would like an explanation, though, because it's completely broken. I'm broken, Lee. You have broken me."

I actually keeled over in half as if I had literally been broken in two.

"Baby, I'm sorry." Lee went to touch me, but I didn't want his touch. I needed his touch. I needed to be comforted, but I didn't want him to touch me. He was the one who had me in so much pain, so how crazy was it that I wanted him to be the antidote to the pain? I pushed his hand away.

After finally finding the strength to straighten myself out, I stood and looked into Lee's eyes. "Do you see me, Lee?"

"Of course I see you, baby. And I could kick myself for some of the decisions I made. I wasn't thinking on that level. I can honestly admit that—"

"No, I mean do you see me . . . or do you see those women? Those women whose pictures you subscribe to? Those women whose pictures you like? Because I look nothing like them, Lee. I got a pouch from carrying your kids, not to mention the stretch marks and the little bit of cottage cheese on the back of my legs. So is that why you subscribe to that type of thing? Because you don't like looking at this?" I allowed my hands to run down my body. "So I ask you again. Do you see me, or do you see them . . . when you're making love to me?"

It killed me to ask Lee that question. It killed me to make myself so vulnerable to Lee. On one hand I hated that I had to reveal to him just how much all this bothered me, but on the other hand I felt he needed to know. If a person doesn't know that something they are doing is hurting you, how can they fix it? That was my logic anyway. But why didn't Lee know this would hurt me? Why didn't he just know? And now that he did know, would he fix it?

"I can't believe you asked me that," Lee said as if he was shocked that I'd asked that question; as if he hadn't given me reason to ask it. "When I'm making love to my wife, I'm making love to my wife. I don't need to visualize another woman."

"Then why do you need to sit and stare at your computer at other women?"

He shrugged. "I don't know. I guess I just like that kind of thing. I'm a man."

"A married man. Some things are supposed to change when you take on a wife. You become one with that woman, Lee. We are supposed to be one person. We are supposed to be a 'we'—an 'us.' But you have made me completely obsolete from your world."

"Baby, will you stop it? You are acting like I won't be seen in public with you. It's just a social networking site."

"A social networking site is public. It's a place where you share your life with other people. I'm supposed to be a part of your life, but where am I at? Huh, Lee, where am I at?"

"Where am I at?" he shot back. "I'm here with you." He then mumbled under his breath, "Where am I at," like I had the audacity to ask that question.

"You're at Juanita's house, that's where you're at." Once again, I wish I could have taken a picture of him with that cold, busted look on his face.

"Wha . . . wha . . . what are you talking about?"

"Ya . . . ya . . . you know what I'm talking about," I stuttered, mocking him. "I saw the inbox messages,

Lee. You asked for naked pictures of the woman. You know what size her house is, where she lives. Why do you know these things, Lee?"

He put his head down and shook his head. "It's not what you think, Musik. It's really not." He thought for a moment and then said, "She stays over there on the east side in one of those apartments. You know, the one your cousin used to stay at." He started snapping his fingers as if trying to recall something. "You know—something Creek. One of those places. Next to the Dairy Queen."

"Save that stupid mess for the next chick!" I shouted. "Because I don't even know why I'm bothering to talk to you. I'm not going to get the truth from someone who has been living a lie."

"I haven't been living a lie. I love you. You are my wife. Everybody who knows me knows I have a wife."

"I don't just want to be your wife on paper, Lee. I want to be your wife physically and emotionally. Emotionally more than anything. I need to feel important, wanted, needed, and valued. You have devalued me. A car and a team jersey is worth more to you than me. And you may think it's petty, but it's my emotions and I'm entitled to feel any way about this situation that I want to." I threw my hands up. "How crazy is this? I'm more concerned about how you feel about me—about how important a role I play in your life—than the fact that you've obviously cheated on me with another woman. And that you've cheated on me emotionally with a number of women."

"But I haven't cheated on you."

"Lee, don't frickin' patronize me. Even if you haven't been to Juanita's house, you know her on an intimate enough basis to ask her to send you naked pictures of herself."

"That was just a joke, Musik. I didn't mean it."

"I'm not laughing, Lee. And there was no 'LOL' after your request or with hers. Or let me guess, is it an inside joke at work?"

"Work?" I thought Lee was going to turn blue.

"Yes. I saw a group work picture of you guys on her FI page. I know you work with Juanita in some capacity. And perhaps I should find out myself just what type of work you guys have been doing."

Lee jumped up and grabbed me by both wrists. "No! Don't bring my job into this. Juanita investigates all of our region's accounts. They might get the wrong idea and I could be fired. If I lose my job, we lose my money, health benefits, et cetera . . . Please, don't do this."

I just stood there, staring at Lee, shaking my head. I could hardly see his face because of the overflow of tears in my eyes that were blurring my vision.

"What?" He said it as if he was aggravated with me. Aggravated with my tears.

"I'm standing here bleeding and all you can think about is your job? You don't care about my feelings and making things okay with me. It took me mentioning your job to finally get a reaction out of you. It took me mentioning your job for you to show some concern and emotion. Wow, Lee. That really makes me feel like I mean everything in the world to you."

Lee grabbed his head and began pacing. "Look, you are overreacting. You're being melodramatic. At this point, you don't have to believe me that FI is not that serious to me. It's just something I do with my time. It's an escape."

"An escape from what? From who?"

The more Lee tried to explain himself, the more he kept jabbing me with the shovel he was using to dig himself out of the hole. What was so bad about life that he felt the need to escape?

"I didn't mean it like that. Musik, will you just . . ." His words trailed off in frustration. "Look, I don't even know what to say to you. I can't seem to say anything right. But what I will say is that you will not bring my job into this. It would ruin me."

I broke down crying once again. I was so hurt, mad, and angry. Lee wasn't getting it. He wasn't getting where I was coming from. He honestly had no idea what was so wrong about what he'd done. That scared me more than anything. The fact that he really saw no wrong in what he'd done, to the extent that I did, only meant one thing: that he'd repeat the same things. That he'd hurt me again.

Had Lee just wholeheartedly acknowledged his wrongdoings, that would have given us a better foundation to work things out on and start over. But we were at the point of no return. I couldn't feel and think for this man. I could cook his food, clean his house, take care of his children, and wash his dirty drawers, but I could not think for him.

"You know what, Lee? Just forget it. There is no reason to stand here and do this any longer. For everything I bring up, you are going to have some lame excuse of a comeback that can neither be confirmed or discounted by me. So what I'm going to do is go and get it directly from the horse's mouth."

"What do you mean by that?"

"I'm about to straight-up contact every last one of these broads, and, as far as your job, since you like the Internet so much, get to getting online and filling out applications. Spend some time on Monster.com instead of FaceIt. How about that?"

"Don't do this, Musik," he pleaded.

"It's already done." I got up in his face. "You can forget about that little image you like to portray yourself as to your family, friends, the church, and your coworkers. I'm about to put the real Lee Hampton on blast. All those little inbox messages, I'm turning them into notes and posting them on your page. All those little strippers' pages that you subscribe to will no longer be private. Everybody's going to know the type of thing you like subscribing to. And I can't wait for your job to find out that you request naked pictures from your coworkers. Didn't your company just crack down on anything that could be construed as sexual harassment? Isn't it like immediate termination now?"

"Musik, please don't do that to me."

"*You did it to yourself!*" I screamed at the top of my lungs. "You did it to me," I whimpered. "And now I'm about to do it to you." Payback was a mutha, and at that moment, not only would divorce suffice, but I had to go out of this marriage with a bang—with the last word—with the 'W'.

I ran to get Lee's laptop, which still had his FI account open on it. "Let the embarrassment and humiliation begin," I spat as I started pushing and clicking all the right buttons that would take me to his inbox.

"What are you doing?" Lee asked, almost exhausted.

I didn't answer him. I just kept clicking away. Lee just stood there shaking his head, trying to make me feel crazy. While I typed and clicked Lee just stood there giving me a bunch of "I'm sorry's," how he'd do better, blah, blah, blah. He shut his mouth momentarily and didn't open it again until he saw this sinister look creep across my lips.

"What?" he said.

"In about three seconds you are going to regret ever creating an FI account." I taunted him by placing my finger over a button on the keyboard. "As soon as I push this button, just more than your relationship status will be available for the world to see." I was prepared to put all Lee's FI information that he hadn't wanted me to know about, let alone the world, on full blast. Then I was prepared to file for divorce.

God hated divorce, but there was no way I could stay with this man feeling the way I was feeling now. Betrayed, worthless, not special. Unloved. Not validated. I hear people say all the time that as long as God loves them, that's all that matters. God loving me is very important to me, but it's not the only love I want or need. It's not the only love God wants for us. Otherwise He wouldn't have bothered to create Eve in the first place. Even God uses man to show us His love. Even God knows His children need other people . . . need to be loved by other people.

I want to be loved by my husband, my children, my parents: the people who are supposed to love me in life. I needed Lee's love to validate me as a wife, and I didn't have that. Only a husband can validate his wife's role as a wife. Period.

I hate divorce too. The last thing I want to do is to taint my Christian walk with a divorce. I'll have to bear that cross. I can hear people now whispering, "What could be so bad that she'd divorce her husband?" I don't want to have to explain it with words, so I'll explain it through social networking. "Lee Royce Hampton," I said to him, "the world is about to see you for the jerk you really are. If I had to learn just what a jerk you were through social networking . . . if I had to learn that being married meant nothing to you, then so will everybody else."

With the push of just one button I was about to forward and post information I'd found on his FaceIt page that would put his lying, cheating self on blast. With just the push of one button, I was about to reveal to the world who the real Lee was. On the count of three Lee would suffer the same pain and humiliation I was now feeling. The pain and humiliation he'd caused me.

One, two . . .

"Go ahead, do it," Lee said, causing me to halt from pushing the button. "Put it all out there for the world to see." He sounded so defeated. *Good.*

"I'm glad I have your blessing, because that's exactly what I'm about to do." This was no idle threat either. No bluffing involved. I felt as if nothing could stop me from getting my version of revenge on Lee for what he'd done to me, for the years he'd stolen of my life, for the way he'd erased my life from his own. My finger went to push the key that would be the beginning of many public FI postings that would initiate a domino effect of humiliation and embarrassment for Lee.

Then Lee said something that I had not even taken into consideration.

"Go right ahead," Lee said, "but remember, not only will you be putting me on blast, you'll be putting yourself on blast too."

And with that, he exited the room, giving me a whole lot more to now consider.

Chapter Eight

Threesome—Every Man's Fantasy

Why, before right now, did I not stop to consider how my act of revenge on Lee would not only affect him, but how it will affect me too? It could affect our children. Once something is put out there on the Internet, no matter if I delete it from my computer or not, it's still out there somewhere. Somebody else might save it or forward it or God knows what. It will always exist. *And even a year from now when I'm prayerfully over this whole FI thing, whether I'm still with Lee or not, will I be able to live with it? Will I be able to live with myself knowing that something I did could have an adverse effect on others, including myself, for the rest of our lives?* I was so caught up in the moment in trying to hurt Lee the same way he has me hurting, that I wasn't looking at things on a larger scale.

Will Lee look like the fool for doing things on the Internet that hurt me, or will I look like the fool for showing and telling the whole world what Lee did to me? I'm so confused and so torn. Yet just seconds ago I was so sure.

"God, why am I hurting like this? Why did Lee do this to me?"

As I open my mouth to say something else, instead of words coming out of my mouth, they came into my head. *You did it to yourself!* Those were my own words.

Was I really about to eat my own words? I mean, just because they were in my mouth didn't mean I had to swallow them . . . right?

I got up from the computer and walked into the master bathroom. Standing in front of the mirror I just stared at myself. Finally, it was time I speak the truth to myself. Up until right now, I'd never, ever, never spoken these words out loud, but for the first time I was about to. I needed to. I did not want to wallow in the pain and hurt I was feeling now. I didn't want a Band-Aid and I didn't want a crutch. I wasn't born on the church pew, but I know enough about God to know that He is a healer. Period, point blank. Crutches and Band-Aids are not from God. Those were just a minor relief. God doesn't play around. God heals. In order to take that first step toward healing, I had to admit my truth.

"I knew my husband wasn't my spirit mate when I married him." There I said it. "But I married him anyway . . . even without God's blessing." I said that too. It was the truth.

I knew how bad I wanted the fairytale and I knew Lee just wasn't that type of guy. But I loved him so much I was willing to give up the fairytale. Maybe not give up the fairytale completely, but just do without it for a while; just long enough for Lee to . . . change.

"I'm so stupid!" That was relationship 101: the person who you married is the person who you married. The person who they were before they said, "I do," is the same person after they say, "I do."

Change is not a guarantee. Change is not always for the better either. But if you are marrying a person based upon the hope—a wing and a prayer—that they might change to fit the mold you've created in your own mind and in your own little world, don't do it. You have to be willing to accept the fact and live with the fact that the same person you married today will be the same person tomorrow and forever.

I shouldn't have done it, not when I knew deep down in my heart that Lee and I were soooo different when it came to marriage. My first red flag that I should not have married Lee was when he used to say, "Marriage is just a piece of paper." With him being a man of God, that should have sent up two red flags. Marriage is a holy union. The sanctity of marriage is ordained by God. So to say that God's word is just a piece of paper—something that holds no value— means that the marriage itself, if it ever takes place, will have no value. *So why am I now so surprised that Lee doesn't value our marriage?*

I guess, if I was to be honest with myself, I'm not surprised. I've known it all along. Felt it. I ignored it though. I acted like that feeling didn't exist deep within my gut. The same way I ignored that feeling was the same way I ignored having a conversation about my nuptials with God. To say that God didn't bless my marriage to Lee is perhaps a little extreme. What I mean is that I never sat down and talked to Him to see how He felt about it. To hear what He had to say. Why? I didn't want to hear what God had to say. I knew what He was going to say, or I kind of knew what He might have said. How did I know? Because of that feeling I had. Those of us who are saved and Holy Ghost filled know that sometimes a feeling is more than just a feeling. It's the Holy Spirit rising up in us speaking to us. I didn't listen though.

When God knew I was going to avoid having that conversation called prayer with Him about whether I should marry Lee, He sent His message through the Spirit. I swept that feeling under the rug. I wanted what I wanted, and I wanted Lee. I wanted that man, and Lord have mercy, that's all I got.

Perhaps that didn't come out right. Lee is more than just a man. Lee is a dang good man. He works his butt off. In the fifteen years I've known him, he has only missed seven days of work outside of his vacation days. He stays on top of the bills. We go on trips and he takes the family on nice vacations. He looks out for all his other family members as well. He calls me no fewer than ten times a day just to talk (unless we are having a disagreement). He takes care of himself and is as fine as all get-out. He dresses nice and makes sure the kids and I dress nice. There is a huge list of pluses and just a couple minor negatives: he doesn't know how to make me feel like his wife. He's a family man with other family members, but not in his own home.

He's always walked five steps ahead of me instead of beside me. He'd rather invite one of his boys to a fight party than me, even though boxing is my favorite sport. Even though he doesn't hang out on the streets, when he does go somewhere he never tells me when or where he's going. He just gets dressed, gets up, and goes, sometimes without even saying good-bye. If one of his family members needs a place to stay, even though it's our house, he doesn't ask me for my input at all. He simply says, "So-and-so is coming to stay with us," and that is usually the end of the discussion. When he wants to make a major purchase, he just does it, not stopping to think once about seeking my input (not my permission, just my input).

At the end of the day I know Lee is a grown man, but I just always thought when a person got married it wasn't just about them anymore. I thought that they had to show a level of respect and consideration to their spouse. But instead of Lee doing these things, he just treats me as though I'm . . . invisible.

"I've always been invisible, long before FaceIt ever came along," I finally admit to the person looking back at me in the mirror. FI just rubbed in the fact that I'm invisible. It put it all up in my face, no pun intended.

Now here I was finding myself in a mess that I hadn't even had the courage to go to God and ask Him to bless. And of course what did I want Him to do now? Bless my mess. I might not have turned to God six years ago before saying, "I do," but at least now I had the courage to turn to God before saying, "I don't."

Right here on the bathroom floor, I kneel down and begin to cry out to God. "Lord, I come to you humble and broken. First and foremost I repent to you for not seeking you in the matters of my marriage before now. But I'm here now, Lord."

I begin to pray non-stop before silencing myself to, for the first time ever, hear what God has to say about my marriage. I can't even describe the feeling as God begins to speak to my spirit and relay His words to me. I'm just paraphrasing, but basically God is telling me that He made Adam. He put Adam to sleep and removed his rib in order to form Eve. He basically did surgery on Adam. After the anesthesia wore off, so to speak, God woke up Adam and he was ready to receive Eve into his life.

"You woke your Adam up too early. I wasn't finished with him yet," God spoke into my spirit.

All of a sudden I'm feeling outside of myself as I cry and beat on the bathroom floor just hearing God speak those words to me loud and clear. I feel completely torn up inside. My God was gently letting me know that I had messed up. It didn't matter if Lee had been the head of the church instead of a deacon. It didn't matter how many times Lee cried out, "Holy, holy." God had not been finished with him yet and I hadn't had even one-tenth of the patience of Job to just sit back and wait on God. To wait on God to finish up with Lee. No, I just had to have my Lee, as is.

"Now what, God?" What else can I say? "Now what?"

"Babe, are you all right?" Lee entered the bathroom with a look of heartfelt concern on his face.

As I stared into his eyes I just broke out crying. I was crying because of the decision I know I have to make.

"Please, baby. I'm sorry. I don't want to see you in pain like this knowing that you're feeling this way because of me," he said. "Look, I'll just take down my FI page if that's what you want me to do."

"I want you to be in love with me, Lee! That's what I want." Flesh was hard to tame as I rose up off the floor like the anger that was rising in me. "Don't you get it? At the end of the day it's not about FaceIt.com. It's about finding out that I'm not a part of your life. That nothing about me is worthy of mentioning. That I'm nothing to you! Not a first thought, second, or third."

I've always hated hearing the truth, especially this truth that I'd buried deep within and just went on with life. I'm angry. At myself. At Lee. Just angry; so angry that I feel like throwing things and destroying things. I feel like tearing up and shredding up everything in the house the same way Lee had done to my heart. I really feel as if I'm on the verge of . . . on the verge of . . . losing it.

You did it to yourself. Why does God have to keep reminding me of that? I know why. I was directing all my anger at Lee all the while I hold a great deal of the blame myself. God knows He has to reel me back in with the truth.

Yes, I am partly to blame, but by the same token I feel as though Lee should man up and just admit that he wasn't ready to do the marriage thing. But then I guess in so many ways he had admitted it. But still, he shouldn't have said, "I do," if he really hadn't wanted to. But on the flip side, I knew he was saying, "I do," when he hadn't shown a sign that he really wanted to.

That sudden reminder/conviction was now starting to calm me down. I can't turn back the hands of time. I had taken vows before God without having ever included God in any part of the marriage. Things were about to change. And little did Lee know, this change would be every man's fantasy—a threesome. Yep, you guessed it: Me, him, and God.

Chapter Nine

What's It Gonna Be?

. Once again I find myself on the bathroom floor in tears. Lee was just standing there, staring at me.

Figures, I thought, *he doesn't even know how to comfort—*

My thoughts come to a complete halt when, the next thing I know, Lee is kneeling down on the floor with me. He wraps me in his arms and just holds me. He doesn't say a word. He just holds me and rocks me back and forth.

"I'm so sorry I'm not your fairytale husband, baby."

I look up into Lee's eyes.

"I'm sorry I'm not that dude whose profile picture is him and his girl. I'm sorry I'm not that dude whose entire FI photo albums are nothing but him and his girl. I'm just not that cat," he said sincerely. "I love you. The fact that you are questioning, after all these years, whether I'm in love with you hurts me. And the fact that you need me to tell and show the world means my showing and telling you, which should be most important, isn't enough.

"What you want me to do and how you want me to be as far as relationships, I never saw that coming up with my mom and the men in her life."

"I never saw it in my home either," I counter, "but I knew that's what I wanted for myself."

"And again, I'm sorry I'm not that dude, but, Musik, I'm never going to be that dude. What I can do is be more mindful of your feelings now that I know how you feel about things. I'm going to try my best to put you first—your thoughts and feelings. I am going to try to be a better husband by making you feel worthy, validated, and loved. Am I still going to mess up? Yes, but as long as we communicate and respect each other and how we are, I think we can work through anything. More importantly, as long as we have God in our life, all things are possible. And with that being said, I'm even going to start getting back into church."

I sniff as Lee wipes my tears away with his hand. He then pulls my chin up and says, "Are you going to give me another chance to prove how much I love you? To show you that you are not an afterthought? That you are first and foremost on my mind and in my life? Because I do want this marriage, this life, with you. But if you don't want it, the last thing I want to do is to force you to live a life that's not meant for you."

Oh, the irony of his words. Here it is, he doesn't want to force me to live a life that is not meant for me, but isn't that basically what I'd done to him?

"Did you hear me?" Lee asked after I didn't respond. I nod. "I hear you."

"Then tell me, Musik. What's it gonna be?"

I'm no longer blocked from Lee's FaceIt page. I'm not his FI friend either. As a matter of fact, Lee doesn't even have an FI page anymore. That day in the bathroom when he asked me, "What's it gonna be?" if I would give him another chance, my reply was in the affirmative. He hugged me and said that the first thing he would do was shut down his FaceIt page.

"Lee, honestly, you don't have to shut down your FI page," I'd told him.

"I'm not going to change overnight and I can't deal with the tension of saying or not saying the right thing on FI. I don't want to risk hurting your feelings again or planting seeds of doubt in your mind about whether I love you, am in love with you, or whatever. Working on making you feel validated as my wife is my number one concern right now, not FI or anyone on FI."

Within minutes after making that pledge to me, Lee shut down his FI page. I have to admit, I kind of felt like a kid in the candy store who'd thrown a tantrum and ended up with the biggest lollipop in the store. My true intentions, though, were never to get Lee to shut down his FI page, but it sure didn't hurt our marriage any with it being down.

I'm ready to let go of all that pain and hurt that the whole FI mess stirred up. I just want to enjoy life with my husband and kids.

Some might think, especially a woman who has been in my shoes, that I gave in too easily. That I forgave Lee too quickly or that maybe I shouldn't have forgiven him at all. Some might think I'm stupid and that if I were to catch Lee red-handed in the act of cheating on me that I would be getting what I deserved. That Lee has shown me who he is and that I should believe him. Some might even say that since I no longer wholeheartedly trust him we will never have a healthy relationship.

That last one, though, that's where a person would be wrong. I do whole heartedly trust Lee. I trust that the chances of him screwing me over again, breaking my heart, is fifty-fifty. Those might not be the best odds when it comes to love, but I have two children to consider. They are worth me taking the chance and rolling the dice.

I'm not expecting the worst at all, but I will always be prepared for it. What do I mean by that? I mean that before logging out of Lee's FI account, I managed to forward a lot of the information to my own FI account. I printed out everything and created a nice little file. Remember now, I was heated at the time I was discovering all that information. I was ready to file for divorce and I'd need proof to back up my claims. I'm glad that now divorce is no longer being considered.

I truly believe that Lee is going to put me first—my thoughts and my feelings. I believe he is going to try to be a better husband, the one I deserve, and give me the fairytale. Heck, I was almost so broken to the point where even if the fairytale was a lie, I'd take it. Just never let me find out the truth.

Is that selling myself short? Am I compromising? I honestly don't know. But what I do know is that I'm glad I cooled off and was able to work things out with Lee for the sake of my happiness, our children's, and hopefully Lee's.

I send up prayers every day that this is what Lee truly wants—has always wanted. But Mama didn't raise no fool. While my temper and anger toward Lee might have cooled off, so will that file I created with all Lee's FaceIt dirt. I've labeled the file, in all red caps, REVENGE. I'm not sure how long that file will be on the cooling rack. Prayerfully and with God's will, I'm hoping it will freeze. But what I do know is that if need be, I will pull it off the shelf in a heartbeat and serve it up as is. After all, revenge is best served cold . . .

About the Authors

Sherri L. Lewis is the *Essence* Bestselling author of *The List* (March, 2009), *My Soul Cries Out* (July, 2007), *Dance Into Destiny* (January, 2008), and the highly acclaimed bestselling sequel to *My Soul Cries Out, Selling My Soul* (March, 2010). Sherri's life passion is to express the reality of the Kingdom of God through the arts, including music, dance, films and television and literature; and through sound biblical teaching. Her ministry thrusts include the message of the Kingdom, intimacy with God, intercessory prayer, understanding prophetic ministry, ministering emotional healing, and birthing individuals into their destiny. She lives in Atlanta, Georgia. You may learn more about Sherri and her novels at www.sherrilewis.com.

Rhonda McKnight is the author of the *Black Expressions* Bestselling novels, *Secrets and Lies* (December, 2009) and *An Inconvenient Friend* (August, 2010). *What Kind of Fool* (February, 2012). She is also the owner of *Legacy Editing*, a freelance fiction editing service and *Urban Christian Fiction Today,* a popular Internet site that highlights African American Christian Fiction. Originally from a small coastal town in New Jersey, she's called Atlanta, Georgia home for thirteen years. You may learn more about Rhonda and her novels at her website www.rhondamcknight.net and at www.facebook.com/booksbyrhonda.

About The Author

BLESSEDselling Author E.N. Joy is the writer behind the five-book "New Day Divas" series and the three-book, "Still Divas" series, both coined the "Soap Opera In Print." Formerly writing secular works under the names Joylynn M. Jossel and JOY, this award-winning author enjoys sharing her literary expertise on conference panels across the map. Under the name N. Joy this author penned the children's story, *The Secret Olivia Told Me,* which received the American Library Association Coretta Scott King Honor. Scholastic Books acquired book club rights and the title has sold almost 100,000 copies. Currently, Joy is the executive editor for Urban Christian, an imprint of Urban Books, LLC in which the titles are distributed by Kensington Publishing Corporation. You can visit this author at www.enjoywrites.com.

Notes